BENCH WITH A VIEW

BENCH WITH A VIEW

PARKS PAT MYSTERIES
BOOK ELEVEN

P. D. WORKMAN

 PD WORKMAN

ISBN: 9781774686546 (KDP Paperback)
ISBN: 9781774686560 (KDP Hardcover)
ISBN: 9781774686539 (Large Print)
ISBN: 9781774686553 (Lulu Paperback)
ISBN: 9781774686522 (ePub)
ISBN: 9781774686577 (Accessible Audio)

ALSO BY P.D. WORKMAN

FIND MORE BOOKS AT PDWORKMAN.COM

MYSTERY/SUSPENSE:

Parks Pat Mysteries
Police Procedural Set in Canada
Out with the Sunset
Long Climb to the Top
Dark Water Under the Bridge
Immersed in the View
Skimming Over the Lake
Hazard of the Hills
Knows the Hills
Spanning the Creek
Sanctuary in the Stream
Echoes of the Engine
Bench with a View
Beneath the Icy Depths
Grounded in the Wind (Coming Soon)
Reservoir of Secrets (Coming Soon)
Peril in the Blooms (Coming Soon)

Kenzie Kirsch Medical Thrillers
Unlawful Harvest
Doctored Death
Dosed to Death

AND MORE AT PDWORKMAN.COM

To those laboring against all odds to save souls.

STYLE NOTE

Since my largest readership is in the USA, I have chosen to use US spellings throughout this series. That includes the Americanization of centre to center, even where it is an actual place name, just for consistency's sake. I apologize to my Canadian readers for this.

I have chosen, however, to use Canadian grammar, particularly for Canadian voices. If you see what you think is a grammar error, it may just be Canadian, eh?

CHAPTER ONE

*M*argie really didn't like early morning calls.

The sunrise was so late in the autumn and winter that she really couldn't expect the sun to have risen before she got to every homicide site. But she never could understand people getting up so early to run or walk their dogs, coming across fresh bodies when it was still too early for Margie to drag herself out of bed.

She had been doing better about getting out to run before work herself but, sometimes, she just kept snoozing her alarms until it was too late to get out. She had stumbled across a body herself on one of her early-morning runs, so who was she to criticize anyone else for doing the same thing?

Margie sat up and grabbed her phone from the nightstand. She used her thumb to answer the call and held it to her ear.

"Patenaude."

"I'm looking for Parks Pat," the dispatcher told her cheerfully.

"This is Detective Pat," she acknowledged, trying not to groan. "Does that mean you've got a body in a park?"

"Carburn Park this morning. DB on a park bench."

Margie envisioned a homeless person sleeping on a bench and dying from hypothermia overnight. It had been a mild fall so far, but Calgary weather was not kind to those who preferred to sleep rough.

She covered a yawn before speaking again. "Where is Carburn Park?"

"Not far from you, actually. But it's one of those little gems that is kind of tucked away, and you don't know about it unless it's in your neighborhood or someone tells you about it."

"Okay." Margie cleared her throat. She picked up the water bottle from the nightstand and had a drink. She was not an early-morning person. "I will punch it into my GPS and get there as soon as I can. Tell them I'm on my way."

"Will do, detective."

"Has OCME been called?"

"Yes. They will be behind you. I'm not sure how long you'll have to wait. Take coffee."

"Okay. Thanks."

Margie didn't need to terminate the call; the dispatcher had already hung up. Margie rubbed her eyes. She knew better than to lie back down or even just sit on the edge of the bed waiting until she was fully awake. It was a sure way to fall back asleep.

She went to the bathroom to splash water on her face and quickly do her hair, coiling her long braid on top of her head. She didn't start the coffee machine in the kitchen. It might wake up Christina. Instead, she would stop by Tim's and get a box of coffee for herself and the other professionals already on the scene. She had learned that the Take 12 worked better than taking a tray of filled cups, when she could only carry a few at a time.

"Mom?"

Margie stopped in Christina's bedroom doorway as she left the bathroom.

"Go back to sleep, honey. It's not time yet."

"You got a call?"

"Yeah."

"I'll call you when I get up."

"That would be great. Let me know how you are doing."

Christina murmured a reply and fell back asleep. They had agreed that Margie would not wake her up before leaving when she was called out, but often Christina woke up anyway when she heard Margie getting ready. Christina would get the details when she was up and getting ready for school or riding the bus.

Stella, though, was a different story. However excited the dog was when Margie got home from work or took her for a walk in the morning, she did not stir if Margie got up before seven—a dog after Margie's own heart.

CHAPTER TWO

*W*ith her Take 12 in the footwell of the passenger seat, Margie set up Carburn Park on her GPS and headed out. The electronic voice directed her south on Deerfoot Trail, which was busier than Margie would have expected so early in the morning. But at least she didn't have to contend with rush hour traffic. The drivers of the cars out on the road were happy to let her zoom over the Calf Robe Bridge and down to Glenmore, even without flashing lights.

She didn't need emergency lights or siren to get to a homicide scene. What difference would it make if she arrived five minutes later without a siren? The victim was already dead. The Office of the Chief Medical Examiner death scene investigator would be behind her somewhere, and the other crime scene investigators wouldn't have much reason to be there before it was light and they could see what they were doing properly. It wasn't like a kidnapping or hostage situation where seconds counted. The victim would still be dead when she arrived.

What had looked like a fairly simple route to the park turned out to be a lot of twists and turns, and then, finally, Margie reached the park entrance.

It was right in the middle of a residential area. Probably a lot of walkers liked to take their turn around the park every day or two. Lots of witnesses who could help narrow down the time of death. Though there had probably been only a few walkers out that late or early.

Margie drove in slowly and parked her car with a cluster of other vehicles. A young constable with a traffic wand indicated the direction she should go. "Around the pond here, ma'am. Clockwise is shorter. Just keep hugging the pond on your right. Can't miss it."

Margie could see large lights being set up partway around the pond. She would have to be blind to miss them. "Thank you," she told him and offered the Tim's box. He took a cup and she filled it.

"Thank you!" he said, pulling down his mask to drink and giving her an appreciative grin.

Margie switched the box of coffee from one side to the other as she walked around the pond. It wasn't that heavy, but it got heavier the farther she walked.

As she approached, she studied the scene, brightly lit in the middle of the dark park. It was a strange sight, like a play or tableau with spotlights on it. She had imagined an old man in voluminous coats lying on the park bench, having passed away in his sleep. Not too much to investigate. Just a natural death. Sad, but something that inevitably happened at least once a year in Calgary, usually in the depths of winter when it was 35 or 40 below. Some homeless person sitting in a bus shelter to avoid the wind and snow.

Instead, the victim appeared to be sitting up. As if he were just looking out onto the pond and had fallen asleep, never to wake up again.

As Margie got closer and again switched the Tim's Take 12 from one hand to the other, she realized the victim was a woman rather than a man.

It didn't take long to reach the bench. At her approach, the other law enforcement officers looked up and fell silent. Margie stopped a short distance away to put on protective gear. She wasn't as sure now that it was just someone who had died of hypothermia or passed away in her sleep.

"Here, someone better take this," Margie offered, showing the Tim's coffee. A couple of officers hurried to take it from her and set it on a table with folding legs that had been set up away from the scene. Margie saw a garbage bag that already contained a few discarded coffee cups.

Free of her offering, Margie approached the bench to have a look at the victim.

It looked at first glance as though the woman were merely sleeping on the bench. Her face was at rest, her eyes closed. Her body was leaning slightly to the side but not falling over. As if she might jerk awake at any moment. The bright white lights were not flattering, but she did not have the gray pallor of many of the victims Margie saw. Her skin was a rich golden brown and had not yet taken on the chalkiness Margie expected. She was probably around Margie's age, in her thirties, and was not a homeless person. Her hair and skin were well-cared-for and her overcoat was pristine and good quality. Margie couldn't see the brand and didn't know enough about fashion to immediately identify it, but guessed it was LL Bean or a pricier brand.

"Well, this is not at all what I was expecting," she told the others.

"What were you expecting?" one of the patrol cops asked, taking a sip of the fresh Tim's coffee.

"The dispatcher said a body on a park bench, and I just figured… an old homeless man."

"That'll teach you not to jump to conclusions."

"Do we have a name yet? Does anyone know how long she's been here?"

"No identification yet. But we haven't touched anything other than to make sure that she was dead. Waiting on you and the ME's office."

Margie was not going to go poking through the woman's

pockets either. She would wait until the death investigator had a chance to examine the body in situ and to check her pockets and handbag.

"Does she have a purse?" Margie asked, looking around.

Everyone looked at the woman, under the bench, and scanned the nearby ground.

"Nothing immediately obvious. We'll need to check the bushes and water when it's light out."

"Yeah." Margie took another step back and carefully looked around. There was no sign of the woman's personal possessions. "Is she wearing any jewelry? Watch?"

"You think it was a mugging? Doesn't look like any mugging I've ever seen," disagreed a cop with a short, grizzled beard that showed around his mask.

"No, I'm not making any assumptions. I'm in the information-gathering phase."

Margie stretched medical gloves over her warm gloves and gently pushed back the sleeves and collar of the coat to expose the victim's wrists and throat.

She was wearing a pretty but practical wristwatch. It was not a big name, nothing Margie recognized, and probably the jewels inset in the bezel were nothing more than zircons. No wedding ring on her finger. No necklace.

"No gloves," the younger cop noted.

Margie nodded. "It might be unseasonably warm, but I still wouldn't walk to this side of the pond without gloves, much less sit down to watch the ducks or wait for someone to meet me with bare hands."

She had made sure she had her gloves on before she stepped out of her car and picked up the Tim's box. Had the woman walked over and sat down without gloves? If so, why? Had it been a rush trip and she'd forgotten? Had she dropped them? Had someone taken them? With a jacket like that, she had to have gloves. Probably leather. Real leather, not the synthetic stuff.

Margie made a mental note of the missing purse and gloves.

She didn't want to take off her own gloves to write in her notebook yet; it seemed like it took forever for her fingers to warm up again once they'd gotten good and cold. Policing in the cold weather was not at the top of her list of favorite things to do—especially middle-of-the-night or early-morning callouts.

CHAPTER THREE

*D*o we have any witnesses? Anyone who can tell us how long she's been here?"

"Not yet. Found by early morning walkers. But I don't know how many people walked by here before someone realized she wasn't just resting her eyes. The woman over there is the one who called in." The cop nodded to an older woman standing a short distance away, outside the area that had been cordoned off with yellow tape. She looked cold, but was waiting to see if she needed to answer any other questions.

Although Margie figured there was little she actually needed from the woman, and she'd probably already told the cops who were first to the scene everything she knew, it was best to talk to her anyway. Show her that her opinion was valued and that they were listening to her.

She approached the woman. "Hi. Detective Patenaude. I'm sorry to keep you waiting here. I'm sure you want to get home and get warmed up. How are you doing? Can I grab you a coffee?"

"Oh, no, I'm fine," the older woman said with a gentle smile. "I just wanted to make sure that you had all of the information you need before I go anywhere. I want to be a good citizen."

"I certainly appreciate you calling it in and waiting around to help us out. Why don't we start with you just telling me your story, start to finish, and I'll ask you some questions afterwards."

"Okay. My name is Betty. Betty Mitchell. I walk here most mornings. Got to keep myself in shape, and you don't do that by just sitting around all day. I spend an hour walking every morning, and it does wonders for my health. And helps to keep off those pesky pounds."

"Which is a big health benefit by itself," Margie agreed with a nod. "Funny how the pounds start to pile on any time you let down your guard."

Betty nodded. "Oh, just you wait until menopause." She rolled her eyes. "That's when the battle really begins!"

"Oh, don't tell me that. But I said I wouldn't interrupt. You got here like usual this morning."

"I have a headlamp," Betty tapped the headband light that she had turned off now that they were under the bright police lights. "So it doesn't matter what time of the year it is, I can get out and exercise even if the sun doesn't rise until eight-thirty."

"Good plan."

"I generally go at the same time every day and, when you do that, you get to know the regulars. Even if you don't talk or walk together, you smile and nod and say good morning. You get to know the people and the dogs, since there are always a couple of dogs here."

Margie could see a few lone figures still taking their regular walks, not stopping to gawk at the police, but keeping an eye on what was happening. There were a few walkers with dogs.

"When I walked past the bench the first time, I was a little surprised to see that young woman here. She isn't a regular. And when it is dark, people don't usually sit down to enjoy the pond. They keep moving, unless they have to stop to tie a shoe or something. And with the mornings being so *brisk*, no one stops for long. If you keep moving, you stay warm. She's not dressed to sit down for very long. She would get cold." Betty pressed her lips together and shook her head. "It just didn't seem right. When I made a second circuit of the pond, she was still in exactly the same position, like she'd fallen asleep there and hadn't stirred. It didn't feel right. I was worried about… well, that she could be drunk or maybe diabetic."

"What time do you think you got to the park in the first place?"

"Five-thirty, maybe. Around then. I shook her, tried to get her attention, you know, and she didn't move, and she was stiff…"

"And you knew that she wasn't just having a nap."

"I feel terrible that I did not realize something was wrong the first time and just left her there."

"You couldn't have known. She does not look like most of the bodies that I deal with. I would not say that she has been dead for very long, and her dark complexion keeps her from looking gray."

"You're…" Betty looked at Margie, hesitating as she searched for the appropriate term. The politically correct terminology changed over the years and those who were older and didn't keep track often used words that had fallen out of favor. "You are First Nations yourself, aren't you?"

Margie nodded. "I am," she agreed. "Métis." Even with her mask on, her heritage was obvious. She looked toward the woman sitting on the bench, waiting for someone who would never come. While it was impossible to be absolutely certain, the woman's dark skin, black hair, and high cheekbones made her look Indigenous as well. She had more delicate features than Margie, and might have some Asian influences. She was not from just a white European heritage; that much was certain. "And she looks like she is."

Margie saw a white van approaching from the parking lot down the paved pathway toward them, moving very slowly—the Office of the Chief Medical Examiner.

"That will be our death investigator. So you don't remember seeing the deceased here before?"

"No. I think I would have remembered. She is very attractive. Those of us who are usually walking around the pond in the morning… well, you've just rolled out of bed. Maybe combed your hair before putting on a toque. No makeup. No… fashionable clothes. Just some sweats and walking shoes, maybe a warm shell to keep off the wind as it gets colder."

The deceased woman did look out of place, when Margie thought about it like that. She certainly had not just rolled out of bed and thrown on her comfy workout clothes to go for a walk. Lipstick, maybe some eye shadow, smooth and neat black hair. That pretty overcoat. Margie looked at her feet. No sneakers. Blunt-toed flats, so she hadn't come from a cocktail party. No impossible-to-walk-in spiked heels. But not what one would wear to exercise or walk the dog. Maybe shoes for the office or a casual dinner out with friends.

There was something that seemed familiar about her, but the more Margie concentrated on it, the more ethereal it became, slipping away to hide in the back of her mind. If she ignored it, she was more likely to have a flash of insight later.

"Did you see anyone else that you didn't recognize? Today or sometime in the last few days?"

"No, I don't think so. Not that I remember."

"And did you see anyone else close to this bench? Stopping to look at her, shake her by the arm, roll their eyes at you over someone falling asleep in the park at this time of day?"

"No, everyone was just doing their own thing like usual. Independent of each other, but used to being here around other people. It's safer with more people here." She bit her lip, worrying it. "At least, I always thought it was safe. There's never been any trouble here before."

CHAPTER FOUR

*T*he white van with OCME emblazoned on the side of it pulled up to the edge of the yellow-taped perimeter. Margie put her hand on Betty's arm. "Did you give the constable your contact information?"

"Yes, I gave him everything."

"You can get on with your day, then. I have everything I need for now and, if I have any follow-up questions, I will give you a call."

"Okay, thank you. Good luck... I hope you find out what happened." She cast a glance toward the deceased woman, still looking as if she were just at rest. "Maybe it was natural causes. She just had a seizure or an aneurysm or something. She looks so peaceful. I hope she was just sitting here looking at the pond and then... she was gone."

Margie's heart gave a little squeeze. "I hope so too."

But the missing purse gave her pause. Maybe there was a good explanation. Maybe the woman had everything she needed for a short walk and meditation by the pond in her pockets. The keys to her house nearby. Her phone and wallet.

Maybe it was just something simple and unexpected. Something quick. So that the victim hadn't even known that anything was happening, and then she was just gone.

Margie walked over to the white van as the occupants stepped out. She saw that the death investigator was Dr. Kahn.

"Hello, doctor. You got here pretty quickly. You must not have had anything else to see tonight."

His eyes crinkled in a smile. "No, and I would have been up in another hour anyway, so I even had a good night's sleep. Had to roll this one out of bed," he tilted his head toward the technician who had come with him. "I suspect he was up late partying."

"I was not," the tall young man objected, his voice slightly muffled by his mask. "I was just… working on the computer late."

"Working?" Dr. Kahn challenged.

"Well… I did have a campaign I needed to finish."

"Are you running for mayor or gaming?" Margie asked, laughing.

"I *might* have been gaming."

They all laughed. "Oh, the foibles of youth," Dr. Kahn proclaimed. "One day, you'll discover that sleep is more important to your health and success than all the games or movies, no matter how much you enjoy them."

The doctor's slender assistant shrugged. "I know. But sometimes it… pulls me in."

"Well, let's have a look at our newest case and see what we've got."

Dr. Kahn looked at Margie and raised a brow questioningly, but she didn't fill him in on any details. She wanted to hear what he had to say about the woman and what had happened to her. Without any preconceptions or biases.

The two of them got out soft-sided equipment bags and, after suiting up appropriately, walked over to the victim on the bench.

"A lovely young woman," Dr. Kahn observed, dictating through his lapel mike to the recorder in his pocket. "Thirties, slender build, average height, Indigenous or mixed race. No sign of violence on the face or outer clothing."

His assistant took a large camera from his equipment bag and started snapping pictures, moving around to capture all angles.

Dr. Kahn touched the woman's wrist briefly. "No pulse. Rigor is setting in. Dead for a few hours." He looked at the other man. "Do you need to take any more of her clothing and position before I touch anything?"

"You're good to go, doctor."

Dr. Kahn unbuttoned the woman's overcoat slowly and deliberately, then opened it up.

"Do you think it was natural causes?" Margie couldn't help asking. "An aneurysm or something like that? There is no sign of an external injury."

"Much too early to tell," Kahn told her. "We're just getting started. No blood is apparent from this position. That doesn't preclude me finding any as I examine her. Sometimes cause of death is not immediately obvious."

"No, of course," Margie agreed.

She was glad that it didn't appear to be a violent death, though. Maybe this would be an easy case to close.

Dr. Kahn shone a flashlight on the victim's face, moving it back and forth slowly and looking at it from different angles.

"There may be some residue on the face. Let's get some swabs around her mouth and nose."

They worked together carefully, the technician anticipating Dr. Kahn's needs and supplying him with additional swabs and collection vials.

"Clothing appears to be disturbed," Kahn observed. He turned to the law enforcement officers looking on. "Did anyone touch her? Open the coat to search for identification? Check her neck for a pulse?"

They all looked at each other. Margie shook her head. "Certainly not while I've been here. I touched her sleeves and lapels to check for jewelry. I wore gloves. No one unbuttoned the coat."

Kahn moved back while the technician took more pictures, noting that the woman's clothes under her coat had been pulled around. Margie swallowed as she looked on, wondering whether that was an indication of sexual assault. But she waited for the doctor to do a further examination and give them additional information. After the additional pictures had been taken, Dr. Kahn and the technician carefully removed the overcoat. Then Margie could see what Kahn had been talking about. One of the woman's sleeves was pushed up. Maybe it had just happened when she had put on her coat and not bothered to fix. Sometimes, when Margie pulled on her coat, her sleeves would ride up if she weren't holding on to them. The woman might have been distracted or in a hurry. It might have been as easy as that.

"Injection mark," Dr. Kahn observed, exposing the inner arm at the elbow joint.

"Is she an IV drug user?" Margie questioned in surprise. The woman certainly didn't look like an addict. Not that one could always tell. If the woman were a covert drug user, then she would probably have chosen a less conspicuous place to inject. Between the toes, maybe.

"No, I wouldn't say so," Kahn said. He examined the injection site. "No sign that she has injected any other time recently. No scarring, no tracks."

"She doesn't look like a drug user," Kahn's assistant offered.

"Never make an assumption. Just because she doesn't have open sores or meth mouth, that doesn't mean she's not an addict or occasional drug user."

The younger man nodded seriously. Kahn examined the woman's other arm and all visible skin. "Nothing else stands out on examination in situ. We'll see what we can find on the table in autopsy. Do some tox screens, look for any other signs of IV drug use, any signs of assault or recent activity."

"Does she have a wallet?" Margie asked. "Phone, keys?"

Kahn felt each of the woman's pockets and shook his head. "No, nothing. Probably in her purse." he glanced around. "Wherever that is."

"So someone took her purse after she died."

"Could have been opportunistic. Someone saw the woman asleep or dead, the purse on the bench next to her, and decided to snatch it to see if there was anything valuable in it."

Margie nodded. She looked at the LEOs who were there to preserve the scene. "Chances are, they grabbed anything valuable and tossed the rest. Check nearby garbage cans as well as behind bushes or anything between here and the parking lot." She looked at the pond. "I don't imagine we'll be able to dredge the pond for it but, when the sun comes up, if everybody could take a quick look to see if it is near the shore."

They nodded, but no one moved to do anything just yet. An evidence-collection team would come once it was light.

Margie's phone rang. She pulled it out of her pocket and looked at it. She hadn't realized so much time had passed.

"Hi, honey. *Boon matayn*."

"Hey." Christina yawned loudly. "How's your morning going?"

"Well, it could be worse. It's not thirty below."

"That's good. Where are you?"

"Carburn Park."

"Where's that one?"

"Not far, actually. It's in the southeast, in a neighborhood called Riverbend."

"Any water?"

"A pond, at least. And the river is close by. I can't see it from here. But then, I can't see anything much. It's still dark."

"Yeah. So you're okay?"

"I haven't even been thinking about it."

Christina knew about Margie's irrational fear of water. But Margie was getting used to most of the Calgary parks either being beside the river or having a water feature. She ran around the Valleyview Park pond several times a week and was able to do it without any fear of falling in or anything bad happening to her.

"Good," Christina pronounced. She yawned again. "I'm getting ready for school. Took Stella out, so she's fine, but you might want to stop and see her before you go downtown, if it's on the way."

"Sure, I should be able to do that. How are the arrangements for the Indigenous Fair coming along?"

"I can't believe we're so close now. I keep expecting everything to fall apart. That they'll just cancel it, or all of the performers will come down with COVID or something. Or they'll close the schools again."

"I don't think they're going to close the schools. I think they decided it didn't really help that much the last time, and it put a lot of kids in jeopardy."

"Put them in jeopardy?" Christina repeated skeptically. "How did it put them in jeopardy?"

"Because kids who live in violent homes or with pedophiles were trapped twenty-four hours a day with their abusers, who were at home because they were furloughed or working from home or lost their jobs. There was a huge increase in domestic violence and child trafficking during the lockdown." Margie swallowed. "For some kids, school is their only safe place."

"Oh." Christina's voice was quiet. "I didn't know that."

"Really, only law enforcement was aware of it. And maybe some of the school administrators. It didn't make big news."

"It should have."

"Yes. I think it's important for the public and those making decisions for society to know things like that."

"So you don't think the schools will shut down again because of that."

"Probably not. It would also be a problem if they close the schools without imposing another general lockdown, because if people are still working, they need childcare. And for many people, their only childcare is the school system. What are they supposed to do if the schools close and they still have to work? Leave kids at home alone?"

"Yeah. I guess I can probably stop worrying that they're going to shut down and we won't be able to do the Indigenous Fair."

Christina gave a low chuckle. "I can worry about the other disasters instead. People getting the date wrong. Fire or flood. You know, more realistic things."

"It will turn out okay. Even if it isn't everything you want it to be, it will still be more than what would have been done if you hadn't planned anything."

"Doing something is better than doing nothing."

"Always."

"Okay." Christina sighed. "Getting my coffee and then I'm out of here. Have fun with your body."

CHAPTER FIVE

he forensic techs should be arriving any time," she told the small group of LEOs who remained at the scene. "Let's take a quick look around before they come to see if we can find the purse or any other evidence. Then we'll be able to point out any other areas they need to process."

Now that it was light out, everyone seemed agreeable to walking the area outside of the yellow tape, looking for additional evidence rather than just standing in one place. They had run out of coffee and people were restless.

When the crime scene techs got there half an hour later, they'd had no luck in finding the purse or any other evidence that seemed to relate to the dead woman.

Margie briefed the techs and told them about the missing purse. They talked to Dr. Kahn about the victim, and the techs went to work documenting and seeing what else they could find.

Once the techs had done an initial review, Kahn and his assistant returned to the van to get out body bags and a gurney. They went to work moving the stiff body into the inner and outer body bags to contain any fluids. There was no blood on the bench. Nothing that Margie could see on the back of the coat. She still didn't know what had happened to the woman, but she hadn't been stabbed or shot. Dr. Kahn would have to complete the autopsy and tell them what he found. But it did appear that drugs had been involved somehow, which dashed Margie's hopes that it would be a natural death. Bizarre, but explainable.

Margie looked at the victim one more time before Dr. Kahn and his assistant finished wrapping her up in the body bags and transporting her back to OCME.

There was something so familiar about her. Margie motioned for them to stop before they zipped up the bags, staring at the woman's face and trying to figure out why it seemed so familiar. She motioned to the other LEOs.

"Do any of you recognize her? She seems very familiar to me, and I'm wondering if she is a public figure or something like that. Do you know her face from anywhere?"

Everyone came over and took a long look at the woman's face before shaking their heads and walking away.

"She looks kind of like you," one of the constables offered.

Margie thanked him, but shook her head in irritation. It was a well-known phenomenon that people had trouble recognizing faces across racial barriers. Also known as "all you people look the same" syndrome. The young man saw two Indigenous faces and saw only their similar skin color and black hair, not the finer features that would indicate a familial relationship.

"Sorry," she told Dr. Kahn. "It was worth a try. I'm sure I've seen her somewhere, but I have no idea where. Hopefully, it will come to me."

"I will let you know if we are able to identify her through fingerprints or a missing person report. As soon as we have an identification, I'll get back to you with the name."

"I appreciate that. Thanks."

She watched them finish bundling her up and load the body into the van.

It would be easier to spot any evidence now that it was light.

Still, there was also an increasing number of people walking around the park, and Margie was concerned that their scene wasn't sufficiently protected by the yellow tape. They had the primary area quarantined, but they didn't yet know where the purse had been dumped, or if there were any evidence showing how the victim had arrived or whether anyone else had been with her.

CHAPTER SIX

*E*ven though Margie had been called out in the early morning hours, she did not get into the office until late morning. She had missed the usual morning briefing, but gave the bullpen a quick rundown on the scene she had been at that morning.

"Maybe she was killed by beavers," Cruz suggested, deadpan.

Margie's face heated as the rest of the homicide team laughed. She tried to keep her expression blank.

"Well, I did see a lot of beaver trees and a small dam there," she told him. "I'll talk to MacDonald about having you follow up on that line of investigation. Get you some hip-waders, and you can go right down into the water to talk to them and see if they can lead you to the missing purse."

She liked the mental image of the Filipino detective struggling through the mud and bullrushes in hip waders, playing Dr. Dolittle with the beavers. From the chuckles around the room, others appreciated it as well.

Cruz shook his head. "Oh, Detective Pat," he said, sadly, shaking his head.

"So, no identity on the deceased yet?" Siever asked, trying to get them back on track. He liked things to be done in an orderly way and, like all of the detectives, he was disturbed when they could not identify the victim. He could be very tenacious in chasing down missing information. He had a knack for seeing patterns and identifying missing pieces.

"No, not yet. OCME will be checking for any matching missing person reports, but it wouldn't hurt to have a second set of eyes going over them in case there is a piece of information that doesn't quite seem to fit."

"I can do that. Have you entered her vitals in the workspace?"

"Not yet, I just got in. If you're lucky, Dr. Kahn might have gotten to it already. Otherwise, you'll have to wait just a few minutes for me to catch up and get my notes transferred to the computer."

He nodded. "Fair enough."

Margie turned to Detective Katelyn Jones, her best friend in the unit, who sat at the desk next to hers. Jones pushed a lock of blond hair that had escaped her bobby pins back behind her ear. She opened her mouth to ask a question, then her eyes slid to the side, looking past Margie at someone else.

Margie turned to see who had entered the bullpen. He removed a black mask and smiled at her.

"Oh! Lewis!" It had taken Margie an instant to recognize him. The last time she had seen Lewis, he had been undercover as a homeless man; unshaven, in dirty, worn clothing. It had been a difficult case for him and she hadn't seen him in a few weeks. It was odd to see him in a white shirt now, clean-shaven, smelling like laundry soap and aftershave.

"Wow!" She motioned for him to come into the bullpen and indicated him to the rest of the team. "Guys, this is Lewis Riley. The undercover officer I met on the Sarah Thompson case."

"Oh, the woman who met the train," Cruz said. "And you knew her personally, didn't you? I'm sorry, that must have been a real heartbreak."

"It was," Lewis agreed with a nod. "But... I'm doing my best to move on and to fill my free time with all of the things that I have always planned to do someday. Seize the day and all that. No more putting things off until I have time or am retired."

Cruz nodded. "You're a pretty young fella. I wouldn't recommend waiting for retirement!"

"But you do, you know? You say that someday you'll get around to it. When I'm grown up, I'm going to… When I'm retired and have all the time in the world, I'll take up this hobby or travel to that place. You know how it is. So I'm not doing that anymore."

Margie nodded. "Good for you. But what are you doing here?"

Lewis laughed.

"I didn't mean 'what are you doing here?' I meant… it's nice to see you—what are you doing here?"

"That's okay. I heard about your new homicide this morning, the woman discovered in the park. I wanted to follow up and get some more details about it. And I thought… I wanted to see you again, so I would just come over here instead of calling or emailing."

Margie noticed that he had buried the comment that he wanted to see her again in that statement and her face got warm again, but not in embarrassment this time. She smiled and tried to stay focused on what he had said.

"What do you want to know about it? And what does it have to do with your cases? I have to say, by the way, that you clean up pretty good."

"You like this better than Eau de Garbage?" Lewis teased, motioning to himself.

"Well, just a little, yeah."

"You know that I was stationed in Pearce Estate Park. There has been a faction using parks for meetings or dead drops, so I was keeping an eye on things at Pearce Estate, thinking that it was a pretty good bet based on its proximity to downtown. Others have been watching Prince's Island and other downtown parks. But now I'm wondering if… they managed to misdirect us, or we made some false assumptions. Carburn Park was on the list of parks to check out, but it was further down the list."

Margie's stomach knotted. From the beginning, she had worried that there was more to the woman's death than just an accident or natural causes. It had just not felt right.

"What kind of a 'faction' are we talking about?" she demanded. "And who is 'us'? What department are you working for?"

"Shall we sit...?" Lewis motioned to a spare chair that floated around the bullpen.

Margie sat at her desk and motioned in front of it for him to wheel the chair over.

Seeing that they were sitting down to have a private discussion, the other detectives returned to their own work. Margie would, of course, keep them updated on the case through the shared workspace, morning briefings, and whatever other methods were necessary to keep everyone on the same page.

Lewis sat down and he put an expanding folder he had been carrying under his arm on her desk with a thunk. Documents that might relate to her case? If so, it had just taken a huge leap forward.

"What do you know?" Margie asked. "Please tell me that the woman who died was not a cop. I thought she was familiar, and if she was another undercover cop..."

He looked startled by this question. "Uh, no, not as far as I know. I don't know every undercover cop in the city, but if this was related to our case, I should know all of the UCs, and I'm sure I would have heard if one of them had not reported in."

But they both knew that someone could be killed and her body discovered before anyone knew that she was gone. She could have been on her way home to bed, but was killed before she was missed.

They both pretended this was not the case and the woman could not have been a cop.

"Good," Margie pronounced. "You scared me for a minute there. So tell me what you're investigating."

He glanced around the room to ensure no one was listening. Why would he be concerned about someone listening in from the homicide division? Maybe it was just a reflex—something all undercovers did. Margie had not done any significant undercover work herself. Nothing where she had been in position for days or weeks. A few times when they had needed an Indigenous face to blend in, but only for a few hours.

"I'm from ALERT," he explained. "We are investigating new activity by the Alberta Warriors."

ALERT, the Alberta Law Enforcement Response Teams, was an integrated law enforcement agency that focused on organized crime and included the Special Enforcement Unit that focused on gang-related crime.

Margie's throat tightened. She grabbed the water bottle beside her monitor and took a couple of swallows of the stale, lukewarm water.

She cleared her throat and looked at Lewis with wide eyes. "The Alberta Warriors?"

CHAPTER SEVEN

ou've heard of them?" Lewis asked, taking in her reaction. "Most Alberta law enforcement agencies won't even call the gangs by name. They won't do anything that might 'legitimize' them."

"You think pretending they don't exist makes anything better?" Margie demanded. "You don't *invoke* them by calling them by name."

"That's just the viewpoint here. Don't legitimize them, and you limit their scope. Keep people from giving them any respect or regard."

"Well, I came here from Winnipeg. And trust me, I know all about the Manitoba Warriors." She clenched her jaw.

Lewis nodded slowly. "Yeah. The Alberta Warriors are an offshoot of the Manitoba Warriors. And unfortunately, no less violent."

Margie felt sick. She shook her head. "I thought when I left the Peg I was leaving all that behind."

"You can't escape it. You could go to Yellowknife and still have to deal with organized crime."

Margie shook her head. She wanted to say, "At least they wouldn't be Indigenous gangs," but she was sure they were. Other countries ran their cocaine through the territories, and she was sure that Indigenous criminals facilitated it. As much as she would like to suggest that her people were only victims of crime in Canada, particularly at the hands of organized crime, she knew that the statistics didn't bear her out. Most violent crime against Indigenous people was perpetrated by other Indigenous.

She rubbed her forehead, feeling the fatigue from getting up too early that morning starting to weigh on her.

"So you think that the Alberta Warriors are using Calgary parks as hubs for their business and that the woman killed in Carburn Park might have been the victim of that activity?"

"I can't tell you anything. Since all that I know right now is that there was a death in the park, and that it wasn't a homeless person or someone known to the police in the area. I need you to tell me the details."

Closing her eyes, Margie recounted the basics of the case as succinctly as she could. When she opened her eyes, she saw that Lewis had taken out his notepad and was scribbling down notes about what she had related.

"There wasn't any obvious sign of gang activity," Margie said. "We can go back and look for it, but… I didn't see any gang tags or anything else. We walked the area pretty carefully looking for the victim's purse. I thought it would be in a bush or garbage can nearby. Or thrown in the water. But we didn't turn it up."

"And you don't yet have an identity on the victim."

"No."

"But she did have an injection mark," Lewis mused. "An injection suggests drug and possibly gang involvement."

"She looked as clean-cut as anyone I've ever seen," Margie protested. "She was not an addict or a drug runner. She was not a gang member."

"They can clean up pretty good. They don't all look like the Manitoba Warriors you ran into in Winnipeg."

"No. I'd swear it. She was not involved in a gang."

"But she *was* out of place."

Margie thought about it. "Yeah. Yeah, right from the start, I didn't feel like she belonged there. She wasn't a walker. Most of the people through there... they're walking their dogs, getting some exercise themselves, whatever. But she looked like... an office worker, I guess. White collar. Just home from work. Flat, sensible shoes. Nice looking, but not spikes. Something she could work in. Nice clothes, she could certainly live in the area. Be a neighbor of the park... but I still would have expected her to put on sweats or something comfy before going for a walk in the park."

"She was sitting on the bench. Why? Watching the sunset? Birding?"

"Waiting for someone," Margie guessed.

"What makes you think that?"

"Just because she looked out of place, I guess. Like someone told her, you go here and you wait at such-and-such a time, and so she did and, while she was waiting..." Margie trailed off. "I don't know. It looked like she fell asleep and never woke up. But I know that's not what happened. Someone came along and... gave her an injection and took her purse? It really doesn't make much sense yet."

"No. If she wasn't a drug user, then most likely, someone else injected her. But why? People don't generally go around injecting each other with drugs to kill them."

Margie heard what he had been too polite to say.

"Unless they are in a gang."

Because gang violence didn't make any sense. It was just violence. Violence for the sake of violence. Violence to intimidate. To bully their way to the top. To get what they wanted. It didn't have to be measured or logical. They just did whatever it took to get their way. And an organization like the Manitoba Warriors...

Margie shook her head. She should have known that working in homicide, she would never be completely free of the gangs. She would know about it whenever they were involved in a murder. And there would be gang murders. As long as there were Warriors, there would be murders.

"I'm sorry to have to tell you all of this," Lewis said apologetically. "I wish I could just tell you it had nothing to do with the Warriors. That it was just a random act of violence. That you could walk any park in this city just as safe as could be."

Margie laughed bleakly. "I guess I had kind of thought that I was leaving it all behind. The city streets and parks were perfectly safe. Any homicides that I would be investigating would just be domestic or random. I knew there would be organized crime. I knew there were gangs everywhere. Indigenous gangs included. But I had my own little fantasy where I never had to deal with any of them."

"You're sure that the woman was Indigenous."

"Pretty sure, yeah. Looked like it. I could always be wrong. Maybe she was Asian or some mix that just happened to look Indigenous, but I don't think so."

"And you thought you might know her?"

"Well, I feel like I've seen her somewhere before. Like I've seen her on TV or something. Sometime in the past... I don't know. I can't be much help identifying her."

"Do you get together with groups for... *tribal* stuff?" Lewis turned a little bit pink as he fumbled for the right words. "Like community dinners or dances, stuff for school kids to meet each other..."

"Normally, yes, but we got here during lockdown. Large gatherings have not been permitted. We keep saying that we're going to go to the Native Friendship Center, that we're going to get together with cousins that we haven't seen since we got here, all that kind of thing. But we haven't been able to. My daughter Christina, she's organized an Indigenous Fair at her school, and they're getting a bunch of people to talk about their cultures, perform, make crafts and food..."

"What a great idea. It's important to get to know each other's cultures. And even your own sometimes, if you weren't raised doing cultural things or exposed to your language. A lot of Indigenous kids I meet were never a part of a traditional family, haven't been to a reservation, seen a dance, gone on a hunt..."

Margie nodded. "Some of them have really been deprived of their culture," she agreed. But they were getting off-track. Lewis wasn't interested in the plight of the Indigenous in Canada. He was concerned with stopping an Indigenous gang, breaking up their drug networks, the sex and gun trafficking that went with it hand-in-hand. He wasn't fishing for an invitation to a high school awareness day.

"So, did you meet any of the people that your daughter has been making contact with for this Indigenous Fair?"

"Oh... well, yes, I have. She doesn't drive—or, she can, but she only has her learner's right now, and roads like Seventeenth Avenue and Deerfoot make her nervous. So if she has to go anywhere to meet with anyone, then I drive her."

She thought of Christina sitting on a park bench waiting to meet with someone, while Margie sat in the car waiting for her to have her meeting and come back—thought of her falling asleep on that bench and never waking up.

She shook her head to rid herself of this vision. "So, yes, I've met some of the people she has been talking to about the Indigenous Fair."

"Any chance that the victim was someone your daughter had met with? Or the sister or friend of someone she had met with? Even just someone in the background?"

"Well, I can't say no. Of course it is possible." Margie closed her eyes and tried to picture the victim's face and where she might have seen her. She just kept seeing children or youth groups. Had she been an activity coordinator? A public relations person? Where had Margie seen her?

"I'll have to keep thinking about it. I don't know where I saw her. If I saw her. Maybe she just looks similar to someone that I know. That does happen. Two people who look alike but have no connection."

"Of course. Well, if you identify her, please let me know. And if you find anything in Carburn Park that might relate somehow to the Alberta Warriors or a rival gang. I'll leave this with you." He indicated the expanding folder full of paper. "Don't say we didn't share with you in the spirit of openness and cooperation. ALERT can't function without sharing resources. And we aren't going to solve this murder—if it was murder—without sharing information. You know who to call. My contact information is in there. Or you can call ALERT and ask for me by name. If you want to confirm that I am actually who I say I am."

Margie couldn't imagine anyone who wasn't working for the agency would just walk into the homicide unit and sit down with her for a conversation. The Alberta Warriors didn't plant him there. That kind of thing happened on TV thrillers, not in real life.

CHAPTER EIGHT

*W*hen Lewis left, it was time for lunch and, even though Margie felt like she had just barely arrived, she had to get something to eat. She'd only had coffee for breakfast and hadn't stopped to eat when she had gone home to walk Stella. She should have, but she had wanted to get into the office as quickly as she could to get a good start on her paperwork.

The paperwork was not done, but she was famished.

"I'm going for Subway," she announced to Detective Jones. "You want anything?"

"Meatball sandwich?" Jones returned with a smile. "That would really be awesome. I don't want to stop what I'm working on, but if you're going out anyway…"

"Yeah, sure. Meatball sandwich." She already knew Jones's favorite toppings.

"Great. I'll e-transfer you."

"Anyone else?" Margie raised her voice so that the others could hear. "Subway run."

Cruz and Siever both placed their orders as well, and then Margie was on her way to pick everything up.

❦

AFTER EATING and furiously typing all of the information she could to the shared workspace before she opened Lewis's folder and immersed herself in the information about the Alberta Warriors, Margie made one call to OCME to see if Kahn had been able to come up with anything that hadn't been posted yet. She knew it was a long shot and he would probably be irritated with her for calling before he had anything. But there was always a chance he had something already.

"Office of the Chief Medical Examiner, Dr. Kahn speaking," Kahn's soft, pleasant voice answered.

"Oh, hi, Doctor. This is Detective Patenaude. I know it is too early to know anything, but I wondered if…"

"If I knew anything?"

"Yes," Margie laughed at herself. "Exactly."

"Well, I have not yet had a chance to do much. I can confirm that there were not any apparent injuries. I did full body X-rays as well as gross examination, and we are not looking at blunt force trauma, stabbing, or shooting. There are no external signs of strangulation, though I may look a little further for that if circumstances dictate. However, I do have initial testing on the swabs and blood toxicity, and I would suggest that your girl died of a massive fentanyl overdose."

"Fentanyl."

"A synthetic opioid," Dr. Kahn provided.

"I know what it is. How could I be in law enforcement and not know? I think even elementary school kids know what fentanyl is. But she didn't look like a drug user."

"No. I agree. There are no signs on her body that she is a regular fentanyl user. There are no other injection sites, just the one."

"So… someone else injected her. We're looking at a homicide."

"I think we are looking at a homicide rather than an accident. But my examination and report are not anywhere near complete. I cannot rely on field tests for my final report. Samples have been sent to FCSU to test the blood and hair strand levels and give us a nice report with all the bells and whistles. But the field test strips reacted very quickly and definitively. I would guess that the concentrations are high."

"Which is another reason to suspect that she was given the injection rather than taking it herself."

"Yes. If you decided to experiment with IV fentanyl use, I would expect you to start with a very low dose. Its potency is well known. You know the risk of overdose. So unless you were actually trying to kill yourself..."

Margie thought about the woman's body sitting on the bench, looking out into the water. A peaceful, pleasant scene. Was it possible that something had happened in the woman's life and she *had* decided to commit suicide there? Away from her home so that she wouldn't be discovered by her family. In a familiar, pleasant setting where her last sights and thoughts could be about the beautiful yellow and orange leaves rather than whatever had driven her to the act?

"Do you think it was suicide?"

"I haven't made a finding yet, so I can't tell you my final determination. But... I suspect it was not suicide. I told you that the swabs were also positive. The swabs of her face," he reminded her. "I had thought there was something on her face around her mouth and nose. And the swabs of the skin were positive for fentanyl."

"How would she get fentanyl around her mouth and nose?"

"Because someone forced fentanyl powder into her mouth. She inhaled and ingested it."

"And *then* she was injected?"

"Yes," Kahn's voice was grave, and Margie could imagine his sage nod as he confirmed her understanding. "I would suggest she was accosted, forced to ingest fentanyl and, once she was overcome by the effects, was given another dose by intravenous administration, which resulted in cardiac arrest."

Margie could picture it in her mind—the violence of it.

Someone coming up behind the woman as she was sitting on the bench, putting an arm across her neck and a hand full of fentanyl powder over her mouth, holding her until the fentanyl did its job and incapacitated her. Then, the attacker would only have had to open her coat and pull one arm out of the sleeve in order to inject her.

Then, whoever it was had taken the time to put her arm back through the sleeve, button up her coat, and leave her in a position where she looked like she had just been peacefully staring into the water. With the massive dose of fentanyl, she had probably been dead by the time he had finished adjusting the body.

Why? To make it look like she had died of natural causes? Did he think that they would miss the injection mark and not do an autopsy, but just write it off as a natural death? Was it to prevent people from discovering the death immediately, giving her killer time to stroll around the pond at a leisurely pace without being identified as a threat or suspicious person?

Or was it a warning? If Carburn Park or Calgary parks in general were known as the new stomping grounds for the Alberta Warriors, maybe she was a sign, a warning to others not to cross the gang.

If that were the case, then what had the victim done? How had she crossed the Warriors?

"That's about all I can tell you at the moment, Detective," Kahn advised.

"That's a lot more than I expected. We can start putting together a profile of what happened there and investigate it right away instead of waiting for weeks to get the tox reports back from FCSU and realizing that we should have talked to more people, pulled surveillance video, and all that. This will help to guide the investigation. It obviously was not just a natural death."

"That is correct," he agreed.

"This would have been... quite a violent attack. If other people were nearby, they must have seen what happened, wouldn't you think?"

"I would expect so. Fentanyl overdose is quick but not instantaneous. There would have been a struggle. It would have been difficult to disguise it as a friendly tussle or anything other than what it was. But given the state of rigor mortis, I would suggest that she was killed several hours before she was found at five o'clock. I don't imagine there are many people in the park at two o'clock in the morning."

"No." Margie frowned to herself. What had the woman been doing there in the wee hours of the morning? Like Betty, she would probably have needed a headlamp or flashlight to find her way around safely. It would be isolated. Spooky. She hadn't been attacked in the middle of the afternoon, sunning herself on the park bench while she watched the waterfowl.

"We'll have to see what surveillance video we can get from the park or doorbell cams from residences around the park. Maybe we'll be able to identify when she went to the park and who entered around the same time as she did. I can't believe that there were very many people accessing the park at that time of the day."

"Parks are officially closed from eleven until five. I imagine that if residents noticed unusual activity, they might have reported it to the police or 3-1-1."

Margie nodded and made a note. "I'll need to check that," she agreed.

CHAPTER NINE

*M*argie had already gone home and was working on making supper with Christina when the call came in. The caller ID on her phone was Unknown, which she knew could mean that it was someone else in the department. So she tended to answer the phone even when she wasn't sure who was calling.

"Patenaude."

"Detective Patenaude?"

"Yes, how can I help you?"

"Officer of the Day, ma'am. We've just taken a Missing Person that matches the description of your park victim."

Margie looked at the time. Six o'clock. It was, at least, less than twenty-four hours since the discovery of the body. Longer than she had expected, considering the well-cared-for appearance of the woman, but not long enough to be concerning. The victim obviously had people in her life who cared about her and had quickly noticed that she was not where she was supposed to be.

"Great. Can I get the name and the details of the person who filed the report?"

"Missing is Laura Clothier. Husband Alexander filed the report in the last hour." She gave him the phone number and address of the husband. "Missing Person detective who has been assigned to the case is Amelia Banks. Will you be calling her?"

"Yes, I'll need to coordinate with her. Has she been in contact with the husband already?"

"Just to follow up on the missing person report, let him know she's been assigned."

"Is there a picture of the missing woman?"

"I'll send it to this number?"

"Yes, just text it here. Then I can make sure we're both talking about the same person before we give the husband a heart attack, telling him that his wife is dead."

When she finished the phone call, Margie put her phone down and waited for the picture to be sent.

Something was bothering her.

The name kept echoing in her brain and she was sure she had heard it before. Just like she had been sure she had seen the woman's face before.

She tried to put them together. But her brain just wouldn't cooperate.

Her phone vibrated and the message notification flashed across the screen. Margie tapped the message to bring the picture up.

The picture that Alexander Williams had provided of his wife was much more recognizable than the dead woman's face. It was always more challenging to identify a dead person. The relaxation of the muscles, change in skin tone, and other factors all contributed, Margie knew, to giving anyone who knew the victim a sense of *jamais vu*, the feeling her face was foreign and unfamiliar. Sometimes, loved ones had to rely on birthmarks, tattoos, gaps in the teeth, and other such details to identify a loved one because they seemed so unfamiliar in death. Even a skilled funeral home cosmetologist could not always achieve the level of reality needed for loved ones to recognize the deceased.

But the picture of Laura Clothier in living color was a different story. Her eyes were bright, she had a big smile, and her hair was pulled back in a braid. Margie had not seen her since they were children, but she knew those eyes, that face.

She sat down on one of the kitchen chairs with a thump, misjudging the height of the seat. She stared at the picture of Laura, the name and the face finally connecting.

Laura.

"Mom? Are you okay?"

"I just…" Tears sprang to Margie's eyes and ran down her cheeks. She was too shocked to be able to stop them.

"Mom?" Christina hurried over to her, bent down, put an arm around her shoulder, and looked at the picture on Margie's phone. "What is it? What happened?"

"This is… Laura."

Christina nodded. She rubbed Margie's back in slow circles. "Who is she? A friend of yours?"

Margie swallowed. "A cousin. Yes. We used to get together when I was in Calgary. A long time ago." She wiped at the tears that were tracking down her cheek. "I didn't know her. I didn't recognize her. I thought she looked familiar, but it wasn't until I saw this picture that…"

"You didn't know her where? Did you run into her?"

"She was killed. She was the victim I was called about this morning."

"Oh no!" Christina's voice was sharp with the shock of it. "Oh, no, Mom! I'm so sorry."

Margie grasped her hand. "I know. It's okay. I will be okay. It's not me, it's her husband…"

"She was married?"

"I think she has a child, a little boy. Younger than you." She touched Christina's cheek, trying to dredge up all the details. "Six or seven, I think. Oh, that poor boy."

She tried to stop her eyes from leaking, but the tears continued to come. Christina sat beside her, dragging her chair as close as she could to put her arm around Margie. Worried by all of the sniffling, Stella came over to comfort Margie, putting her head in Margie's lap and licking her hands or face whenever they got close enough to reach.

Margie only allowed herself a few minutes, then cleared her throat and stood up.

"I'll need to go over there to give him the death notification. I won't leave them wondering all night what has happened to her."

"Can't someone else do that?"

"No, I want to do it. He should have a friendly face. Someone who knew her."

"Can I come with you? I don't want you to go by yourself."

"No, you really can't, sweetie. It wouldn't be appropriate for me to bring my daughter."

"But they are family."

"Maybe I could take you back another time, when I am not on duty, and we can talk to them as family. Comfort them. But I need to do this officially first."

Margie was still crying. But it was time to get ahold of herself. She blew her nose and walked around the house a bit, trying to get her emotions back under control. She couldn't cry at a death notification. She had a cold glass of water, which helped. She held the cold glass to her hot forehead and looked at the contents of the fridge. They still needed to eat, but she didn't have the time to make something. She needed to eat quickly and get over to Alexander Clothier's house.

CHAPTER TEN

*M*argie focused on following her GPS instructions back to Riverbend to find the Clothier home. With something to do, it was easier to stay in control. But she still wasn't sure how she would manage when it came to breaking the news to Alexander. Would it be easier for him if the news came from a family member, or would it make it harder? Sometimes, the next of kin felt the need to attack the person who delivered the news. To shout at and abuse her because they didn't want to believe it. Because it was such a terrible injustice.

She had given the Missing Persons detective, Amelia Banks, a bare outline of the circumstances of Laura Clothier's death in the park and the fact that she had known Laura years ago and wanted to be the one to break the news to Alexander. But Banks had still wanted to come along. Even though the missing person file would only be open for no more than a couple of hours, she wanted to do her part.

A car pulled in across the street from the Clothier home, and Margie waited for a moment before getting out to see if it was the Missing Persons detective. The woman who got out of that car and looked around was clearly not a resident, but was there to visit or meet someone. To meet Margie and pay a visit to Alexander.

They met in the street to nod to each other briefly, avoiding shaking hands.

"Are you sure you want to do this?" Banks inquired, giving her an out if she wanted to take it. "You don't have to be the one. I can tell them that we have tentatively identified the victim in the park as his wife and then get confirmation with DNA or dental."

"No. He should know that it is more definitive than that. I know her. I recognize her. I know her face and her name. We'll still do a positive ID based on science, but he should be allowed to put his doubts to rest. Hope is not a solace in this situation."

She thought of the little boy. His life was also about to change forever.

They walked toward the house with its porch light on and living room still brightly lit. The door opened as they walked up to the house. Of course Alexander was watching the door. Waiting for his wife to return home. Unaware of the news he was about to get.

"Mr. Clothier?" Banks inquired, holding out her hand.

"No, no. Clothier is my wife's name. I'm Alexander Williams. She kept her name." His eyes drifted to Margie's face. "She was very proud of her heritage."

Margie nodded. She felt bad that they were wearing masks. She wanted him to see her face. To know how she felt when she told him the news. She didn't want to be a faceless monster.

"Oh, I'm sorry. I'm Detective Amelia Banks. This is Detective Patenaude. We're here to follow up on your missing person report. Can we come in?"

He stepped back, opening the door wider and motioning them in. Relieved, Margie thought. He was relieved that they were there, taking his report seriously. That maybe it meant they would be able to find his wife and bring her home to him.

"Let's sit down," Banks suggested gently. The living room was spotless. Margie wondered whether it always looked that way or whether Alexander had cleaned it while he waited for someone to show up, needing something to do to keep himself busy.

It was a nice little bungalow, a single-family home, probably three or four bedrooms. Just the right size for a family to grow into. But that would never happen for Laura now.

"Did you have questions?" Alexander asked. "I have more pictures. The woman at the police station said that they only needed one, but I have more. It was hard to pick out just one that you would be able to recognize her from. I don't know what else to tell you about where to look... I guess you can call the hospitals. They keep telling me they can't give me any information for privacy reasons. Especially if there is anyone who hasn't been identified. How do they expect to be able to identify anyone if they won't tell you details?" He shook his head.

"No, we don't need any other information, Mr. Williams." Banks looked at Margie, inviting her to give the notification now that they were all sitting down.

Margie nodded and cleared her throat.

"Mr. Williams... I'm sorry to tell you that your wife's body was found in Carburn Park early this morning. She had been attacked. She did not survive the assault."

She waited as Alexander tried to process these unexpected words. It was a shock, though he had surely been wondering what could have happened to her. Why hadn't she come home? Why wouldn't she answer the phone? How could she just disappear and not tell anyone where she had gone? He had surely already decided in his own mind that she had either been killed or kidnapped, because what else would have kept her away from her family?

Even if he had been expecting to hear at some point that she had been injured or killed, that didn't make it easy to hear. It didn't make it any easier to reconcile himself to the truth that he was now alone. No longer coupled. Left to raise their child on his own.

"How can that be?" he asked, bewildered.

"We're still trying to sort it all out," Margie said. "I understand that it's difficult to understand. I am a homicide detective, and I will be working on your wife's case. Doing everything I can to bring the people responsible for this to justice."

"People?"

Margie nodded. "We don't yet know who or why. I hope you'll be patient while we investigate. These things often seem like they are taking an inordinate length of time. Even when you know who the killer is in a case, it can still take years to bring them to justice."

"Years? Do you know who did this? I don't understand. How could she be dead? Attacked in the park? Who would do that?"

"We are looking into it. We already have leads we are following up. This is going to be a very difficult time for you. I want you to know that you can call me anytime." Margie already had out her business card and handed it to him. "And… I'm very sorry, Mr. Williams. I want you to know… I knew your wife a long time ago."

His eyes widened. "You knew Laura?" He sat up straighter, looking down at the card, holding it at arm's length like he was farsighted. "Patenaude." His eyes flicked to her face. "Can you take your mask off? I don't think we need them on here. There's plenty of air circulation."

Margie and Banks took their masks off. Margie saw Banks's face for the first time. Firm lips. Soft eyes. Worry lines on her forehead and around her mouth. She looked older than Margie. Most detectives were older than she was.

Alexander barely gave Banks a glance. He studied Margie's face, cataloging her skin tone and features. Margie swallowed.

"Laura was my cousin," Margie explained. "I used to see her when I came here from Winnipeg over the summer. We played together as little children. Explored the city as teens." She licked her dry lips. "We kind of fell out of touch when I stopped coming to Calgary. I had my daughter and needed to get my life in order. I wish I had gotten back in contact with her when we moved to Calgary, but it was in the middle of the lockdown and I didn't do anything more than let people know that I was moving here."

His expression brightened a little, as if this were familiar. "Yes. Yes, I remember her saying that one of her cousins was moving to Calgary and that maybe when all of this stuff was over..." He made a gesture indicating the mask Margie held in her hand. "When this all settled down, maybe she would be able to get together with her. You."

"I'm sorry that didn't happen. I wish we hadn't put it off."

He nodded slowly. "She would have enjoyed it, I'm sure. She always spoke fondly of her cousins."

Margie nodded. She didn't know what else to say, and just sat there in the growing silence, trying to think of what a person was supposed to talk about when she found out that her estranged cousin had been murdered. All of the things that she usually said to the victim's family seemed to fall short.

"She would be happy you're running the investigation," Alexander suggested.

"I don't know. Would she? Maybe she would rather that it was someone else, outside the family. Someone unbiased, with no emotional involvement."

"No. She'd be glad it was you. She was proud of her cousin, the police detective."

"Really?"

He nodded seriously. He looked around, his hands moving restlessly like he needed to pick things up and tidy his surroundings, to occupy himself with something that was needful. But there was nothing left to tidy. He made an effort to fold his hands quietly in his lap. He took a deep breath and let it out. He didn't cry. That would come later. He was too much in the "disbelief" stage now.

"So, tell me what you know and what you need to know from me," he said practically. If he couldn't clean, maybe he could help with the investigation.

CHAPTER ELEVEN

I can't tell you very much yet," Margie said. "Let's start with a few questions. What was it that Laura did? I thought I remembered from social media that she was a social worker?"

Alexander nodded. "That was her training. What she was doing most recently was supervising at a halfway house. She liked to be home with Quinn when he wasn't at school, so she worked nights at the halfway house, just making sure that everyone was where they were supposed to be and someone was there if there was a problem."

Margie nodded. She was aware of nurses, police officers, and others who preferred to take the night shift so that they were available for their kids during the day. Getting enough sleep was a perpetual problem, but that was probably true of most parents.

"What was her shift? How did your schedule work?"

"She took the morning shift. Three until ten. I work nine to five. So I was here in the morning when Quinn would wake up, and I would get him off to school. Then Laura was available if there were any problems with school and was home when he got off. She slept while he was at school, unless something came up. We would have supper and the evening together. She would be able to put Quinn to bed and watch a movie with me. I would go to bed, and she would have a couple of hours to herself before going to work again."

He shook his head and rubbed the center of his forehead tenderly.

"It's a very strange schedule, I know, but it worked for us. She was able to sleep during the day. One of us was always here for Quinn. If he woke up with the flu, I would call in to the office and let them know I would be late, and she would leave early if there were enough people to cover at the halfway house. The only time we overlapped was a couple of hours in the morning."

"That sounds really creative. Laura was an outside-the-box thinker."

Alexander nodded. "It seemed like it worked so much better for us than both working during the day and having to find after-school care."

"So were you aware of Laura going to Carburn Park between when you went to bed and her going to work? Was that a regular thing?"

"She sometimes went over there... I wouldn't say I liked it. I knew it was closed and she could get in trouble for being there. And it was so isolated. She said that was what she liked about it. She could be there all by herself, like it was her own little sanctuary." He sniffled and wiped his nose. "I said that we had a perfectly good garden and fishpond in the backyard, and she could sit there, and I would be much happier about her safety."

They all chuckled a bit about it, even knowing it had ended tragically. What if Laura had listened to her husband and just sat in the backyard when she wanted some time to think and meditate in nature?

But Margie knew that wouldn't be the same. For Laura, as with Margie, being in nature meant more than sitting in the backyard. Even the parks were a compromise. Finding something in the city that would do. They both remembered what it was really like in the wilds. When Kokum and Moushoom or someone else

49

in the family would gather all of the kids together and take them out onto Crown Land or the reservation. Where things were really wild and untouched. They could learn how to watch and listen for the animals, follow a trail, and learn about the different plants and trees and their medicinal properties.

Margie had lost so much of that knowledge in the years since Christina was born. She was just returning to her roots now, getting Moushoom to teach her some of the things that she should know. And teaching them to Christina, so that she wasn't a complete city girl, but knew a bit about how to live with nature.

And as far as following a trail and learning how to orient herself in the wilderness… Margie had been hopeless at that part. She had absolutely no sense of direction, something that had sent Laura into peals of laughter time after time. Margie getting lost on family outings in Calgary was a regular occurrence. She knew her surroundings a bit better in Winnipeg, but they had never spent much time in the wilderness in Manitoba. In the city, she knew her streets and could find her way home or ask for directions. There were only a few wild places they ever went to, and Margie learned them the best she could and stuck like glue to her mother or one of her aunties if there were any chance of her getting lost out there.

"So as I said, that's where she was when it happened," Margie said apologetically. "In one of her favorite places. Being one with Mother Earth."

"It was just random?" Alexander asked. "She never even ran into anyone out there. It was just… the deer and the night birds, the splash of the beavers in the water. Sometimes, she told me what she saw there but, usually, there wasn't anything exciting to announce. It was just… a good place to get centered before going to work."

"She would want to have that before going to a halfway house. What was it like? What kind of offenders was she dealing with?"

"It was a juvenile halfway house. So she wasn't dealing with hardened adult offenders. Kids who had served their time and needed something to help integrate back into society. She called them her kids. She was really close to them. A lot of young offenders are Indigenous. Forty to fifty percent of them. I guess I don't have to tell you that."

Margie's chest tightened as she nodded. It was one of the reasons that it had been so important to get Christina out of Winnipeg, where violent crime was the highest of anywhere in Canada, with the majority of the victims and the offenders being Indigenous. Calgary was better, but still bad. As much as she wanted Christina to be part of the Indigenous community in Calgary, she was actually happy that she didn't have many Indigenous friends, and those she did have did not seem to be in gangs or any trouble.

But that didn't stop an obviously Indian teen from being picked up just for walking down the street, with charges that started with loitering, increased to resisting arrest when she protested, and escalated to assault if she tried to defend herself. In a few minutes, a dark-skinned, black-haired, obviously Indigenous girl like Christina could go from being a model citizen to a violent offender.

"Had she ever run into any trouble at the halfway house? Threats? Violence from any of the participants?"

"Some of that is bound to go on," Alexander admitted. "I was always worried about it. But Laura said I didn't have anything to worry about. They were good kids; they just needed help getting settled in and integrated back into society."

"What were their stats like? Reintegration and recidivism? Did the kids get out and stay out, or…?"

"You would have to look it up or ask them. I don't actually know. They had successes. But I know that a lot of kids went back into the system, either while they were at the house or shortly after."

Margie and Banks both nodded. The odds were not great that someone who had been incarcerated for a few years, especially at a young age, would stay out of the system for that long. Once the damage was done, it was hard to get them back on a productive path, and to help them to stay there.

"How did..." Alexander started. "I mean... how did it happen? Did they...? I mean... out there in the dark where it was so isolated? I suppose that they were just after one thing."

Margie held up her hand, shaking her head. "No," she assured him. "No sign of sexual assault. It was a very strange case and we are doing our best to unwind it so that we can figure out what prompted the attack, if anything. It was actually a drug overdose." She saw Alexander open his mouth to protest, the anger tightening in his face. "We know she wasn't an addict. We know she wasn't using. It was a forced overdose. And we don't know why."

He sat there just looking at her. Margie tried to read his face. His dark eyes and skin glistened in the lamplight.

"I'll do my best to find out why, as well as who. But sometimes, it is just random violence."

Alexander nodded mutely. Banks made movements like it was time to go, but Margie was not ready.

"What would Laura have had with her?"

"With her?"

"What possessions? I assume she carried a purse, wallet, cell phone..."

"Yes. Of course. Keys. A little breakfast to eat while she was there. She could have eaten breakfast with the residents, but she said that they had so little funding, she didn't want to take food out of the mouths of her kids. Sometimes, she took food *to* them. She'd make a big batch of cinnamon buns or peanut butter cookies and spoil them. She said that someone needed to show them some love."

Margie smiled at her cousin's generosity. She had seen some social workers and group home or halfway house supervisors who were very hard. Bitter and disillusioned. When they found out that the system didn't work the way that it was supposed to and that kids kept getting hurt and offenders kept reoffending, the compassion fizzled out and they built up walls to protect themselves. Laura was the other kind. The kind who just kept doing more and never stopped caring.

"Do you track her phone?"

Alexander blinked at her. "No."

"Do you have friend locations or 'find my phone,' or any of these other apps that would tell you where her phone is now? Or earlier in the day?"

"I don't know." Alexander pulled out his phone and looked at it. "I'm pretty useless at these things."

"Can I see?"

He unlocked it and passed it over to her. Margie wasn't a big techie either. She got Christina to show her how to do things on her phone, or played with the settings until something either started working or broke. But she knew enough to start searching for apps that shared locations and might show the location of Laura's phone. In all likelihood, it was at the bottom of the pond and would never work again. It wouldn't lead them directly to the killer's lair. But sometimes criminals were stupid. Killers were *frequently* stupid. A stolen iPad or phone had led the police to a thief or killer more than once in the past.

CHAPTER TWELVE

*S*crolling through screens, Margie managed to find Alexander's *Find My* app, which, if they were lucky, would be set up to find the other devices in the household, including Laura's phone. Since Alexander was not familiar with the app, it was just as likely that she would not be able to find anything with it, that it would think it was alone in the world. But she still held out a little hope. Devices were smarter and smarter and, if she were lucky, the phone would know what other devices were regularly logged in to its home network and would have been granted permission from Laura's phone to track its location in case it was lost or stolen.

She waited while the splash screen appeared and things whirred in the background. A map appeared on the screen, and *Finding your devices* was superimposed over it as a status report. Then, several triangles appeared on the map.

Laura's Phone

Margie tapped on the icon. It wasn't far away, and she was afraid that the last known location would be the home's WIFI network. It wouldn't help her much if the last time Laura's phone had made contact with her cloud account had been when she was at home. She might not have background location tracking turned on.

Margie knew that location tracking could be turned on and off easily enough. Christina had granted Margie location tracking on her phone but, sometimes, when Margie tried to see where Christina was when she was late coming home or just wanted to make sure she had gotten to school safely, her phone was unreachable. She never knew whether it was a network issue or if Christina had intentionally blocked the transmission of her location so that she could sneak off somewhere.

Kids did that. It was completely normal for kids to want their privacy and not be tracked constantly. They needed to explore and test their boundaries in order to grow more independent and self-sufficient.

That didn't mean she had to like it.

Margie zoomed in. The last location of the phone had been that morning just after three o'clock. Which was after the time that Laura would have gone to the park. Her work at the halfway house started at three, so she would have gone to the park an hour or more before that.

And she had not left the park until OCME had transported her body later that morning.

She waited for the background map to resolve. It looked like a residential street between the park and the house. Maybe thrown into a garbage can or some bushes. Margie tapped the triangle to obtain a GPS reading and then dialed Siever's number on her own phone.

"Detective Siever," he answered, sounding vague and far away.

"Patenaude," Margie said briskly. "I need you to look up some map coordinates for me."

"What? Okay." Siever returned to the real world, coming to attention. He was a techie at heart. Anything involving computers or devices was his wheelhouse and would be far more interesting to him than touchy-feely human nature or relationship stuff.

Margie read the coordinates to him. She could hear Siever tapping the numbers into his computer as she read them out.

"Okay," he said, confirming that he'd gotten the location. He read the address it was closest to. "What do you want me to do?"

"That is the last known location of Laura Clothier's phone. We need to get someone over there to look for it. Looks to me like it was probably dumped there. It isn't showing up as inside the house—probably the yard or a garbage can. And you never know when a garbage can is going to be emptied. It will be easier to find it while it is still on the street than in the municipal dump."

"Who is Laura Clothier?"

"Oh—the identity of our Carburn Park victim. Sorry. She was just identified in the last hour."

"Laura Clothier," Siever repeated, trying to embed it in his memory. He agreed. "Sure, I'll call it in. Maybe… I'll head over there and see if I can find anything myself. It's dark, so getting a team out there isn't going to happen until the sun is up tomorrow."

Margie looked at the window, remembering that it was after supper. It was nighttime. She must have reached Siever at home.

"Oh, sheesh. I lost track of the time," she told him apologetically. "I was thinking I was getting you at the office. You don't need to do this tonight. Yes, in the morning, once the sun is out, will have to do. Garbage pickup isn't likely to be before that."

Even though the garbage trucks frequently reached Margie's house before dawn. She pushed that thought aside. She needed to be reasonable. Some things just were not going to happen on her timetable.

"It's okay," Siever said. "I wasn't doing anything that can't be put aside. I'll go over there. I probably won't find anything, but it's worth checking out. If I don't find anything, I'll get a team looking in the morning. If I do, then we can have the tech guys working on it as soon as they open in the morning."

It probably pained him that he couldn't be the one to force the phone to give up its secrets. But the detectives were supposed to leave that for the techies to do in a way that no evidence was destroyed. That involved things like dumping the internal memory of the phone onto a computer and manipulating it there, rather than directly on the phone, so that no data could be accidentally overwritten. Siever could check if there were any messages on the lock screen of the phone, as long as he didn't touch them. And maybe he could discern something from the state of Laura's purse and its contents, if the purse and the phone were still together.

"I really appreciate that," she told Siever sincerely. He was going out of his way to help with the case. While they all worked long hours in the beginning of a case, checking out clues as quickly as possible, he wasn't obligated to drop his evening plans to look for a phone in the dark, when chances were he would find nothing.

"No problem. Where are you?"

"With the family. Just grabbed the location from her husband's phone. Last contact with Laura's phone was at three this morning."

He grunted. "Might still be there. I'll see if I can find anything."

"Thank you."

She disconnected the call. Putting down Alexander's phone, she took a couple of pictures with her own phone to document the information, then handed it back to him.

"Thanks. We'll probably subpoena that information from the cloud service as well, but these things take time, and it is good to act on it as quickly as possible. I appreciate that."

Alexander nodded. His eyes were misty. He was far away, probably thinking about his wife and how his life was going to be totally different from that point in time forward.

"I wonder if I could also take a look around here," Margie said gently. "See if there is anything to indicate trouble in Laura's life. The possibility that she was aware of a crime, or a threat had been made, or anything like that."

Frown lines appeared between Alexander's eyebrows.

"Yes… of course." He shook his head as if trying to clear the mental fog. "Do you mean… that it was targeted? That this wasn't just some random mugging?"

Margie nodded. "Someone forcibly administered a drug overdose," she reminded him. "That isn't a mugging. We think it was related to a gang."

"A gang?" He shook his head. "We don't have gangs around here. In this neighborhood. This is a good neighborhood."

"I'm sure it is. And that there isn't a lot of violence to worry about. But there are gangs in Calgary, and ALERT has been aware of gang activity in some other Calgary parks, so we need to take that into account in our investigation. And since there isn't reason for a gang to target a woman sitting on a park bench randomly, we have to investigate the possible reasons for the attack."

Alexander stared off into space, and Margie thought she had lost him. It wasn't the right time to explain their theories. He couldn't take it in right now.

"You can look around," he said slowly. "Whatever you want, of course. But the house was already searched."

Margie's heart pounded. She looked at Banks, startled and wanting to make sure she had heard correctly. Banks looked just as surprised as Margie felt.

"What do you mean it was already searched?"

"Quinn called me at work when he got home because he couldn't get into the house. I called Laura and couldn't get an answer. I was really worried. But I thought she might still be asleep and just hadn't woken up when he rang the doorbell. Or maybe she had the flu. Quinn has a key, but Laura usually gets up and has the door unlocked for him and he doesn't have to use it. So he called me, crying that she didn't open the door. I got him to let himself in with his key… and she wasn't here. I was home in… fifteen minutes, maybe." He gave her an embarrassed look. "I might have broken a couple of speed limits on the way. When I got home, I looked around and couldn't figure out what Quinn had been looking for." He made a gesture to indicate the house around them. "Drawers were open. Some papers scattered around. It wasn't like on TV when someone's house gets tossed and there are ripped sheets and upholstery slashed and everything overturned. Not like that. But someone had been looking for something…"

"And you thought it was Quinn."

"Yes… but he said he wasn't. He said it must have been Laura. That she had been looking for something, and then she'd had to leave. And she forgot that he was coming home from school." Alexander shrugged and shook his head. "We were both very upset. I was trying to keep him calm and not let him see how concerned I was about her being gone. He felt abandoned because she wasn't there to let him in and take care of him, so he was trying to make up a scenario that explained it."

"And did you think that he was the one who had left everything open? Or that it was Laura?"

"I don't know." Alexander blinked a few times as if trying to remember something that had happened a long time ago. "Nothing made sense to me. So I was just trying to… make everything normal. I closed the drawers while I made Quinn an afterschool snack, like Laura would have done. I didn't go through anything or try to figure it out. I was…"

"You were in shock. You were afraid that something terrible had happened. You didn't want it to be true. So you just continued as if it was normal."

"Yes… something like that. I picked up any papers or anything that had been disturbed, and I took the dishes out of the dishwasher and started to think about supper. I called Laura a few times, but couldn't get her. I didn't want Quinn to see how worried I was, so I didn't call her too many times in front of him and I didn't call the police to report her missing until after supper when he was off playing on his computer. I know you're supposed to wait twenty-four hours, but…"

"No, you don't need to wait twenty-four hours. You knew her

schedule and that she wasn't where she was supposed to be. That something was wrong or she would have been here for Quinn. You did the right thing."

"Do you think so?" he asked, sounding pitiful.

"I wouldn't have been able to identify her if you hadn't."

He looked surprised. "She's your cousin."

"I know, but I haven't seen her since we were kids, and it's harder when…" she trailed off and shrugged. She didn't want to explain to him how corpses looked different from live people. He didn't need to think about that. "You did the right thing," she repeated. "It would have delayed our investigation if you had waited. Now I have a line on the possible location of her phone and purse. I can take a quick look around here for anything that might give us a clue of if she had been getting threats or hiding something. And I can follow up with the halfway house to see if there is any possibility that this is related to her work."

"I don't see how it could be anything other than… just bad luck."

"Don't worry about that. That part is my job. You have enough to worry about. You let me sort out what happened."

He shrugged and looked away from her. Margie hated to think about the list of jobs that he had to do with his wife dead and a young son to raise on his own. At least it wasn't like it had been a hundred years ago, when a man left to raise children himself would more than likely have to parcel them off to neighbors or relatives. There were lots of single dads. There were ways for him to do it. His son was at school during the day and, if he needed to put in extra hours, maybe he could do so remotely after the boy was asleep.

She rose to her feet. "I'll just look around, if you don't mind. Do you want to walk through and tell me what drawers were open and what things you picked up and put away?"

"I don't know if I can remember everything. It was kind of a mess and I was panicking."

"Just tell me what you can remember. Any little thing might

help. If you remember something else in the next few days, you can call me and tell me. There's no pressure for you to remember right now."

He nodded. Banks didn't know what else to do, so she tagged along with them, listening in and looking around. Maybe something would catch her eye and she could contribute to the investigation. Otherwise, her role in the case was over. The missing person had been found. Her case would just funnel into the homicide case.

CHAPTER THIRTEEN

*A*lexander pointed out various drawers that had been pulled out. All of the top drawers in the kitchen, the drawers in a writing desk, and the top drawer in a bureau of the bedroom. Nothing in Quinn's room or the guest room. Alexander couldn't remember for sure what papers had been on the floor, and Margie paged through all of the papers on the counter by the back door, which appeared to be where the family's mail was generally deposited, and the writing desk.

Alexander blinked and looked around, frowning. "Did Laura take her computer to work with her? She must have, but she didn't usually."

"Her laptop is missing?"

"Yes."

"What about yours?"

He considered for a moment. "No. I had mine at work. But also… the tablet. Unless Quinn has it."

"Do you want to see?" she prompted him.

Alexander was reluctant to do so, but eventually nodded. He knocked on Quinn's door and then opened it to peek in.

"Mom?" Margie heard Quinn inquire immediately, his high

child's voice piercing. Then he saw that it was only his father. "Oh, Dad. Did Mom answer her phone yet?"

Margie could see him through the door. Older than she had remembered. She had put him at five or six, but a glance showed he was older. Eight or even ten. His mother's high cheekbones. Two slender braids. Dressed in a black band t-shirt and jeans.

"No, sorry, bud," Alexander told him. "They... we'll talk about it later. I was looking for the tablet. Do you have it?"

"No, I'm playing on my computer."

"Have you seen it? Who had it last?"

"I dunno."

Alexander stood there for a moment longer, but Quinn, apparently absorbed in his game, didn't make any suggestions. Alexander withdrew, shutting the door again.

"I don't know what to say to him," he told Margie. "I don't know when to tell him or what to say."

"If you want, I can do it."

Alexander shook his head immediately. "Oh, no. That wouldn't be good at all. Laura would never agree to that. It's my responsibility. It would be terrible coming from a stranger."

"Then... maybe after we're gone, ask him to come have a bowl of ice cream with you when he's done his game. Then... just tell him gently, but clearly. Don't use phrases that could be construed more than one way. Don't say 'she's gone' or 'they found her body.' Say 'she's dead' so that he doesn't wonder what it really means or hope that she'll come back."

Alexander put both hands over his face, covering up a grimace of grief. He stood there for a minute like that, and Margie waited for the tears and sobs, for the breakdown. But he eventually lowered his hands again, face composed.

"Thank you. That helps."

Margie didn't find anything unusual in Laura's writing desk or bedroom. The mail waiting to be dealt with consisted of household bills, subscriptions, and routine stuff everyone had. A notice from the CRA that no one wanted to open.

Alexander couldn't identify anything else that was missing or anything else that had been out of place when he got home. She hoped he would get through the night okay.

"Is there anyone you can call to stay with you? So the house doesn't feel so empty? In case you want to talk about it?"

Alexander shook his head. "I don't have any family here—only Laura's. And as far as friends, they're all work colleagues. I'm going to have to call them tomorrow and tell them. I'd rather be on my own tonight."

"You have my card. If you need to talk…"

He nodded. "Thanks."

"I'm family. You can call me anytime, even at two in the morning. I take middle-of-the-night calls."

"Okay. I'll have Quinn tonight. He'll probably want to sleep in our bed anyway."

Margie said a reluctant goodbye, and she and Banks walked out together.

SHE WAS in her car when Siever called back.

"I found it," he announced proudly.

"You found the phone? That's fantastic! Good job, Detective."

She wished she could see Siever's face, since he didn't say anything to acknowledge this. She hoped that he didn't think she was being patronizing, because that hadn't been her intention. She was delighted that he had managed to find the evidence..

"Tell me all about it. Was it in a garbage can?"

"Yeah, a bin for collection out on the street, so I assume the truck will be around in the morning. Good thing we acted on your instinct and followed up on it tonight."

"Wow. Good. And was it just the phone, or the purse too?"

"Purse too. I've commandeered the bin and I'm having it picked up. I'd take it in myself, but I've just got a little car."

Margie remembered a recent trip in her car with a shopping cart hanging out of the trunk and understood his problem. They should all drive pick-ups. Little compact cars were great on gas, but not so great for moving larger items.

"The techs should be the ones collecting it anyway. You don't want to obscure any fingerprint evidence. There might be fingerprints on the inside of the handholds."

"I wore gloves. Can't promise I didn't smear anything, but I did my best. I pulled the phone out, but I left everything else in place. Looks like the contents of the purse were dumped, and I didn't want to lose any trace evidence on the little bits."

"Wallet?"

"It's in there."

"So they didn't want the wallet or the phone."

"I didn't open the wallet. Don't know if they took her cash and credit cards. That's all they usually want. Not the wallet itself or any of your reward cards or ID."

"No, you're right. I guess we'll hear tomorrow what all is in there. Anything unusual on the lock screen of the phone?"

"Just dozens of calls and texts from the husband. Appointments that hadn't been cleared. A few other calls, but I don't know what they are. After they are processed, we might have some people to interview."

"Great. I'll check in at her work tomorrow. And someone has been through the house."

"Oh?" Siever sounded surprised or interested, or maybe both.

"The husband had already straightened up, but the top drawers of the kitchen and bureau and the writing desk had been opened. And a laptop and iPad are missing."

"They were looking for electronics," Siever deduced immediately. "Maybe a thumb drive."

"I was thinking that too."

"Hmm. So she was killed because of something she knew? Something she had written down or saved somewhere."

"Certainly looks that way."

"Why did they ditch the phone, then?" Siever mused.

"Whatever they were looking for wasn't on it."

"How did they know?"

He sucked on his teeth. "Must have unlocked it."

"How?"

"Fingerprint or face scan."

Margie grimaced, thinking of the attacker pressing Laura's thumb to the phone screen before or shortly after she died. From what Margie understood from the medical examiner, it was easier to get a fingerprint scan on a conductive screen from a live body than a dead one. She supposed whoever had killed her knew that, too. The fingerprint scan had probably been done after he had incapacitated her, before he killed her with the injection.

This case was going to give her nightmares for sure. She tried not to think about Laura and how close they had once been. How could anyone kill such a bright spirit? Laura was one of those people who was always more concerned about other people than herself, who reached out the first time she thought someone might need a boost, and who never tried to raise herself up over anyone else.

Why did it have to be Laura?

She cleared her throat and tried to speak without giving her emotion away to Siever. Though he was one of those people who didn't always get nuance.

"I need to hang up now to drive. Thanks so much for finding the phone and purse. I hope you don't have to wait too long for the bin to be picked up."

Margie knew she should probably drive the few blocks to meet him and wait with him, but she needed to get back to Christina.

"That's okay. My car is warm and my phone is charged. I can sit here comfortably for a couple of hours."

"I owe you one."

He disconnected without any further comment. Margie nodded to herself. That was just like him. She wiped her eyes, pretending to herself that the burning was just fatigue. It had been a long day that had started very early. Fifteen minutes to drive home, and then she could head to bed if she wanted to. If she thought she would be able to sleep.

But she might just as easily be spending the night in front of the TV, waiting for the fatigue to do its job.

CHAPTER FOURTEEN

*M*argie had consumed a couple of cups of strong coffee before heading to Second Step, the halfway house where Laura had worked. She knew that the coffee did all kinds of bad things to her digestion, but it was her preferred delivery vehicle for caffeine. Wake-up tablets were not nearly as tasty. Hopefully, after putting in a full day's work, her brain and her body would decide that they'd had enough and she could go to sleep.

She certainly wasn't the first homicide detective to pull an all-nighter. Though she wished she had been more productive the previous sleepless night. There hadn't been much to do other than worry about the case and process whatever memories she could of Laura.

None of which was particularly helpful. Whatever they had done together as children when Margie came to Calgary on summer vacations had nothing to do with whoever who had ended Laura's life.

They had not been involved in anything remotely related to gangs, not the Alberta Warriors or any other street gang or an unofficial group of similarly aged children. They hadn't been born into families that were already part of the gangs. They hadn't hung out with gang kids or been recruited by older kids to participate in any activities.

Maybe that was why Laura had ended up where she had, a social worker helping kids leaving juvie to find their place in the community. She had been able to stay out of the gangs, so she had what it took to help other kids back into a normal life.

She had always had a strong affinity for good and had always been a rule follower. Not someone that Margie's mother had ever worried would lead her astray. Margie's summers in Calgary had influenced her life positively, not negatively. They hadn't kept her from making any wrong choices, but it had helped. Maybe that was why Margie had brought Christina to Calgary.

She rang the doorbell at Second Step, and she and Lewis stood there waiting for someone to answer. It wasn't unexpected that it took a lot of yelling back and forth between residents before someone was eventually harassed into answering the door. In a place like that, it was always someone else's job to answer the door, and everybody was too busy.

The door opened three inches and a slim, Indigenous young man stood on the inside looking out at Margie, ready to shut the door again if it were someone trying to sell a natural gas plan.

"Detectives Patenaude and Riley. Here to see Angie Craig," Margie advised.

The boy looked back over his shoulder. "Missus Craig?"

Margie couldn't make out whether there was an answering shout.

"Somebody here," he shouted. "Couple cops."

If they expected an uproar over the fact that there were cops at the door—displays of fear, panic, or guilt—they were disappointed. No one seemed to care. Eventually, the boy stepped back, pulling the door open the rest of the way.

"I guess you may as well come in," he conceded.

Margie and Lewis entered the house.

It was about what Margie had expected. Carpet worn almost through to the floorboards. The stale smell of cigarette smoke, even though she was sure the house probably had rules about not smoking in the house. Combined with old cooking smells, onions and chili. Lots of people on the move, talking to each other, negotiating with the supervisors, doing chores. Furniture nearly as worn as the carpets.

"Could you get Mrs. Craig or direct us to her office?"

"Uh... yeah, sure. She's just back there," he pointed toward the back right corner of the house.

He drifted away from them.

"Thank you," Margie called after him.

Lewis chuckled. They found their way to the bedroom the boy had pointed to, finding that it had been transformed into several office cubicles, all of them too small for a meeting.

"We're looking for Mrs. Craig?"

A woman with masses of gray hair working at a computer looked at them.

"Oh, are you the detectives? I'm sorry, I didn't know you were here. I hope you haven't been waiting long."

"Is there somewhere we can talk?" Margie suggested.

"Well..." Angie Craig looked around. "Not really anywhere private. Maybe... we should go for a walk."

So, back outside they went. Margie had left her hat and gloves in the car, expecting to be inside the warm house. She burrowed her hands down into her pockets and hoped they would keep up a brisk enough pace to keep warm.

"I was... I was so sorry to hear about Laura," Mrs. Craig said. "I don't know what to think. What a horrible thing to happen. Crazy."

"She was supposed to be here at three?"

"Yes, that's right. When Laura didn't get here, we left a few messages on her phone. Couldn't get through to her. I thought maybe her phone service was out. Probably home with a sick kid and..." Mrs. Craig trailed off. "I couldn't find something to explain it all satisfactorily, I guess, because if she was staying home with Quinn, she would have called one of us, explained what was going on, and ensured we had someone to cover for her. She was always very considerate. She never just… failed to show up. I said it was nothing, but I was worried."

"You didn't feel the need to report her absence?"

"To who?" Mrs. Craig mused. "Her husband?"

"A supervisor. I don't know how things work here. Maybe someone, when they couldn't reach her, might try the police. Ask them to do a welfare check."

Mrs. Craig shook her head. "That all seems a little… intrusive."

"You weren't worried enough to follow up on it?"

"We were floundering to cover for her. Dealing with everything here. It isn't easy to get coverage at three in the morning. She left us in the lurch. I mean, now I know that she didn't, but at the time, how were we to know the difference? We couldn't stop to worry about that. We needed to make sure that everyone was supervised and everyone's needs were met."

Margie nodded. It was a small organization. Just a few supervisors trying to cover all of the shifts. Laura's failure to show up for her shift had been more of an inconvenience than something they needed to deal with. It wasn't unusual for a workplace to be the first to report a missing person to the police. But it usually took a few days. Someone who didn't have a spouse or other family members in the home.

"Can you tell me what Laura did here?"

"The same as any of us do. Keep an eye on things. Make sure that the kids are complying with their release requirements. Report those who aren't. Help them enroll in school, find jobs, find places to live when they are ready to transition out of here. And then… be a sort of a den mother as well. Break up fights. Teach kids how to communicate with each other. Coping skills. Life skills. Get them referrals to doctors, help them keep track of their meds. Be a listening ear."

Laura would have been good at that. Margie had been surprised that she only had one child; Laura was the sort of person she would have expected to have a whole house full of kids. And she had. It just happened to be a halfway house rather than her own.

"How long had Laura worked here?"

"Oh, she's an old hand... Maybe five years? I would have to check her employment records. She wasn't a newbie. A lot of people bounce after a few days or a few weeks. It just isn't what they expected it to be, or they find that they can't handle it for one reason or another. Laura was steady. She was born to this kind of work."

"Had she had any problems lately? Conflicts with any of the kids? Trouble at home? Any... outside threats?"

"Nothing unusual, no."

Margie waited, letting Mrs. Craig think about it. Her answer had been too quick.

"She had been... I don't know if the right word is depressed. She seemed more moody than usual. Not quite as patient as usual. But people do burn out. She'd been here for a long time. She might have felt like it was time to move on to something else."

"Had she talked to you about that?"

"No, no. I just thought she seemed a little stressed. A little... moody."

"Did she talk about something that had happened to worry her? Even if it wasn't related to the kids here. Something that was on her mind. Distracting her."

"She didn't say what it was. But..." Mrs. Craig looked around, as if expecting someone to be listening in on them. "There was Patrick Belcourt. Laura seemed to be talking to him a lot lately. I wondered what was going on with him, but she didn't draw anything to the attention of the staff about him. And Ceci McKay. She said that we needed to keep an eye on Ceci. She didn't say why."

"What are their histories? Patrick and Ceci?"

Mrs. Craig was hesitant to disclose anything. "Well, I suppose you have access to their criminal files..."

Margie nodded. They didn't always have the access they wanted to young offender files, but they could ask for court orders to have them disclosed. If they were pertinent to the case. If they were worried that the youths might be a danger to others. If there was evidence they might have had something to do with Laura's death. It was a stretch. Much easier if Mrs. Craig just filled them in on what she had been told.

"Well... Patrick is Métis and Cec is Blackfoot." She nodded toward Margie as if to emphasize their Indigenous heritage in case they didn't understand. "They both had very rough upbringings. A lot of... I don't want to say neglect, but many of these families don't really know how to parent or how to provide for their children. It is a legacy they have struggled with for generations. We break up families and then expect them to know how to be families." She shrugged. It was not something she had personally done to them, not something she could change. Just one of the facts of life she had to deal with at the halfway house.

"And their charges?"

"Patrick... assault and gross bodily harm. Cec, a number of drug charges. She had a very long history of stuff she had served little or no time for in the past, and then a judge got tired of it. Decided to really hit her and make her realize she couldn't continue to go on that way. So she ended up serving four years."

A long time for a youthful offender.

"Personal drug use, or...?"

"She was dealing. Probably started out with running drugs for a family member as a child. By the time she was old enough to charge, she was well into the business. But a sweet little thing who could charm cops and judges and convince them that she would change her ways if they just gave her one more chance."

She could probably no longer masquerade as a sweet little thing after four years of prison time.

"And Laura was spending a lot of time with these two?"

"Not a lot. But... maybe more than the other kids. She was closer to them."

"Because they were Indigenous?"

"More than half of our kids are. There seemed to be something about these two in particular that had drawn Laura's attention."

None of them said anything for a minute, walking and thinking.

"Gang affiliations?" Lewis asked finally.

Mrs. Craig raised her head to look at him. "Gang affiliations?" she repeated.

"Do you know their gang affiliations?"

Mrs. Craig didn't say anything at first. Maybe she wanted to deny that they had any affiliation or that anyone in the house knew anything about it. Margie was surprised that Lewis had asked the question so directly, but she was quiet, trusting that he knew what he was doing. She didn't want to get in his way.

"Alberta Warriors," Mrs. Craig said finally. "Both of them."

CHAPTER FIFTEEN

*L*ewis took the lead in questioning Patrick. He was a tall, loose-limbed Indigenous youth with an acne-pocked face who looked at them warily and was not inclined to trust them. He did raise his brows, however, at the fact that Margie was also Indigenous.

"I don't know any Indian cops," he said. "I didn't know there were any. Other than the ones on the rez, and they are useless, you know? No one wants to talk to them and they're either acting all high and mighty over everyone or joining you for a drink and pretending that they are just one of the guys and not looking to narc on you or bring you before the council."

"There aren't a lot of us," Margie admitted. "I really wish that there were more. I think that it would be easier to address Indigenous issues if there were more Indigenous cops. But the fact that our own people are not likely to listen to us and just see us as Oreos or traitors... that makes it pretty hard to have the effect we would like to on the community."

"Indians don't belong on the police force."

Margie shrugged. "Maybe not. But I'm not giving up any time soon."

He nodded slowly.

"So… we're here because of Laura Clothier," Lewis inserted, not interested in a philosophical discussion of Indigenous bands self-policing. They had an actual case to investigate. A dead woman. A widowed husband and motherless child. Those things were real and concrete, and were what they needed to focus on.

Patrick looked genuinely saddened at the mention of Laura's name. "I heard about that," he said, shaking his head. "That is bad business." His eyes drooped halfway, hooded, not looking at either of them. "Mrs. Clothier was a good person. She really cared about the kids here."

He looked around for a moment, identifying anyone who might be close enough to overhear the conversation. "Not all the adults here care. Some of them…" He trailed off, thinking about it. "It's complicated." He rubbed the bridge of his nose. "But Mrs. Clothier was solid."

Margie and Lewis nodded. Margie waited to see if he would offer anything else without prompting.

"Did you hear anything about how she died?" she asked eventually.

Patrick cleared his throat. "No."

It was clearly a lie. Margie and Lewis waited for him to consider his answer and confirm or deny it.

"I heard it was, like, a mugging," Patrick said eventually, bouncing his leg nervously. "Like, she was in the park after dark, and she got ambushed, and they took her stuff. I don't know why she was there, and she wouldn't carry around a lot of cash or something late at night in the middle of the park. She's just coming here; she doesn't spend anything when she's here."

"She wasn't mugged," Margie told him. "This wasn't someone who held her up and she fought back or the mugger got too jumpy. This was a targeted attack. A premeditated murder."

"No… that couldn't be." He pressed his lips together, frowning worriedly. "No one would do that to Mrs. Clothier."

"I think she knew something," Lewis said. His voice had an

edge to it. A toughness that Patrick would know from prison. "And I think it was to do with the Alberta Warriors."

Patrick swallowed.

"I understand you're with the Alberta Warriors," Lewis said. "So maybe you can tell me what it was about."

Patrick was too late to hide the AW tattoo on the back of one hand and 1-23 on the back of the other. Margie didn't know if he would have hidden them if he could. The ink declared his affiliation to anyone who knew them, and hiding it would have been pointless. He'd chosen to make that affiliation public and couldn't take it back now.

"I don't know of any beef the Warriors have—had—with Mrs. Clothier. Why would they care anything about a halfway house night supervisor? You can't get much *smaller* than that."

"She was killed in AW territory with a fentanyl overdose," Margie said. "Do you really think that could lead us to any other conclusion?"

"Fentanyl?" Patrick swallowed and wiped his mouth with the back of his hand. "Why would they do that?"

"I think they wanted to make it known that she was interfering where she wasn't wanted," Lewis contributed. "Where she had no business being. As a warning to anyone else who tried to get in the middle of gang business."

"What could she get in the way of? What could she know?" Patrick protested.

"Maybe you can tell us," Margie suggested. "You're AW and you were in close contact with her. Maybe you said something to her. Or maybe you had something to do with her murder."

"I never! I wouldn't do anything to hurt her. I told you, she was good to us. She helped to protect us and to help us get on the right track. She didn't want us in gangs. So maybe they didn't like her trying to take kids away from the gang, but she didn't make enough of a difference for them to care. What difference do one or two kids make to the organization?"

"You haven't heard anything through the grapevine? About

why she was killed? You never said anything to anyone that might have set off alarm bells?"

"I would *never* do or say anything that would get her hurt," he protested.

"You're loyal to the Warriors, aren't you?" Lewis pressed. "If you had to prove your loyalty to them, you would turn on anyone you had to. And that includes a lowly nighttime supervisor at your halfway house."

"I'm loyal... but I would never let them do anything to hurt her. If I knew... I would have warned her."

"Maybe you didn't know beforehand," Lewis said, "But you know now. Aren't you going to do anything to avenge her murder? Help bring her killer to justice?"

Patrick's face was a mask. It was all hard, unfeeling planes. "I can't do that," he told them. "I can't go against the Warriors."

"That's what I figured," Lewis said. "You say that you liked Mrs. Clothier and that she's good people, but when it comes down to it, you really don't care. Your little gang is more important to you than anything that happened to her. You don't care about the people you took her away from. Her husband. Her little boy. Do you know what it is like to lose your mother when you're just a little boy?"

Patrick cleared his throat. He scratched at a pimple on his cheek. "Yeah, I do."

"But you just don't care. Too bad for him."

"I can't change it. I can't take it back and give her back to him. Doesn't matter how bad I feel about it, she's still going to be dead and he's still not going to have a mom."

"You can stop them from killing someone else. You can let them know that justice has been served."

"I can't do anything about it."

"You could tell us who killed her. Who ordered it. You knew her. You knew who she was in contact with through this house. If you didn't have anything to do with it, then it was likely someone else in the house. So step up. Be a man. Look after your own."

Patrick looked around. "I can't talk. I can't tell you anything. They know who I am. They would know if I talked. You think I want to go out that way too?" He shook his head. "Actually, they wouldn't kill a traitor that way. That was a nice way to go for someone like her. A traitor…" He trailed off and let them think about how the Alberta Warriors would deal with a traitor. Someone they knew had talked. Torture him? Cut out his tongue? A long, painful death. Maybe, in the end, the mercy of a slit throat. Everyone would know that he had betrayed his gang. His family. His community.

How many more people in the house were Alberta Warriors? They hadn't asked Mrs. Craig. She probably would have been able to tell them. Most of them, anyway. There would always be those who didn't talk about their affiliation but remained loyal to a faction behind the scenes.

"Patrick. We can take you in," Margie told him. "You don't need to talk here. We can take you in on some charge and you can tell us in the police station, where no one will overhear you and no word can get back to the gang."

He looked at her for a minute, maybe even considering it, but in the end, he shook his head again. "I can't," he told her, his voice strained.

"She was my cousin," Margie told him. "A sister to me. You killed my sister."

He swallowed hard, his Adam's apple bobbing up and down. "I didn't have anything to do with it. I swear."

"Your family killed her. Your gang killed her. That makes you guilty of it, too."

He shook his head wordlessly, eyes glistening. But he didn't break down and tell them who the responsible party had been.

CHAPTER SIXTEEN

*I*f Lewis thought Ceci would be easier to question because she was a girl...

Margie knew that Ceci would be that much harder. She knew gang girls. And she knew how they used their feminine wiles to make their interrogators think that they were frail or vulnerable. She knew how fake and underhanded they could be, hiding their true natures behind smiles and simpers and begging for help. Then, when they walked away, they would laugh with their girls about how easy men were to manipulate.

So Margie wouldn't let Lewis take the lead in the discussion with Ceci. Ceci who had a long, long list of charges before a judge had finally seen through her act and cracked down on her.

Ceci was not the nice little girl that Mrs. Craig had described, who had been able to charm cops and judges. As Margie had expected, she had changed during her years in prison. Margie could still see the outer shell that had fooled people in the past, but the Ceci she saw now had a hard face, piercing black eyes, and the smooth movements and caution of a feral cat.

She was a product of the prison system. It sounded like she had a family history with the gang as well, or at last with the drug trade, so she had probably been hard before prison.

"Hi, Ceci. Can I call you that? I'm Detective Pat."

Ceci nodded uncaringly. "Call me whatever you like."

"I wanted to talk to you because of what happened to Laura Clothier. She was my family." Margie said it in a hard, flat tone. Staking out her territory. *Alberta Warriors killed my family.* So Ceci would know that she had a real stake in this.

Ceci looked surprised. She played with a stud in her lip.

"I didn't know Mrs. Clothier had family here."

"Did you know she was married? That she had a little boy?"

Ceci looked away. She wrapped a long lock of hair around her finger and let it go again, repeatedly.

"Well, yeah. Everybody has somebody," she said eventually.

"Not everybody has a ten-year-old boy who has to grow up without a mother now."

"I don't even know why you're talking to me. Do you think I had something to do with her getting killed? Look at the check-in sheet; I was here, just like I'm supposed to be, before curfew. We can't sneak out of here to go murder someone." She pulled on the lock of hair. Long and hard so that it made Margie wince. Ceci leaned forward. "And if I wanted to kill her, why would I go to the park? She was coming here."

"I don't think that you killed her directly. But I think your gang did, and that's the same thing."

"I didn't have anything to do with it."

"Tell me who did."

Ceci laughed. "Even if I knew, do you think I could tell you? You think I want to be killed, too?"

"Why target Laura? She was a good person. She was here to help you. She called you all her kids, and I understand she gave you special attention. Why would you just stand by and say nothing while your gang killed her? Why would you let them get away with it?"

"What makes you think it was Alberta Warriors?"

It was Lewis who answered. "I have been undercover at the parks for months. I know which gangs are involved. I know that she was killed by the Alberta Warriors. I'm not sure why—probably over a drug shipment, considering the way she was killed. The question is, what did she know that could get her killed?"

Ceci sat back in her chair, arms folded across her chest. "What do I know? I'm here to rehabilitate, you know. To transition from prison to respectable society. Mrs. Clothier didn't want us associating with anyone from the Warriors."

"And so you didn't?" Lewis questioned, his face twisting into a sneer. "You never talked to anyone from the Warriors? Do you know how ridiculous that sounds?"

She didn't like being mocked and told that she sounded ridiculous. No one, especially a tough gang girl, wanted to look ridiculous in front of others, even if they were strangers.

"I can't help talking to anyone in the gang," she pointed out. "Not when they're in my own house."

Margie and Lewis sat there looking at her. She knew that she had said too much, but it was too late to take it back, and trying would just make her look weak. So instead, she tried to bluff her way through it.

"AW is everywhere you go," she told Lewis. "She knows," Ceci jutted her chin at Margie. "You can't get away from them. They're in every prison, every community, every family. And I'm not going to blab to the police and have them take action against me."

"So you'd rather that Mrs. Clothier's killer just went free."

"I wasn't the one who hurt her. I wouldn't have ever done that." Ceci looked at Margie, and her hard expression melted slightly, her chin quivering just a bit. "She was really your family? Your cousin? You're not just saying that?"

"Yes. My cousin. I lived in Winnipeg, and I used to come to Calgary during the summer, and she and I would spend days together. Exploring the city, having a fun time, going to Cochrane for ice cream with Moushoom. She was so…" Margie struggled to think of the right word. "So nurturing. I don't mean she was like a mother, because she wasn't. But she was just… ready to be my best friend, someone I could always call on. Someone who always buoyed me up."

Ceci nodded. "She was like that."

"Was she to you too? I'm glad. She was a special person, and Alexander told me how much she loved 'her kids' here. You were her family too. She chose to spend the time with you."

"It was her job," Ceci said dismissively.

"It wasn't just her job. She could have done a lot of things. You think that someone like her had nothing else she could do? That was the only thing she could find? She didn't need to be babysitting juvies. She *chose* to be here. But you and the others… you're acting like none of that mattered. I guess she didn't mean anything to any of you. You think what AW did was okay. Maybe you think she deserved it for sticking her nose into someone else's business." Margie leaned forward and slowed down her speech, trying to emphasize each word. "But you know she was trying to help you."

Ceci looked away, blinking. She shook her head. "She got herself into trouble. It was nothing to do with me. I wouldn't have turned her in. I'd never have betrayed her."

"But you'll betray her memory. You'll let her little son spend the rest of his life wondering who killed his mother and why nobody cared enough to stop it or to tell the police what had happened."

"She was in the park," Ceci said.

"Yes."

"She knew it wasn't safe there."

"She was in the park near her house, where she always went to walk or think. Why should that be dangerous for her? She was on her way here. Just stopping to look at the frozen pond for a few minutes. To meditate and get her head on straight so that she would be one hundred percent there for you and the others. Even if you were sleeping, she still wanted to make sure that she had done everything she could to prepare herself. Take that extra few minutes."

Ceci shook her head. "She wasn't sitting on that bench to meditate."

"What, then?"

"She thought she could stop them. She was stupid. One person can't stop the Warriors. She should have stayed out of it."

"What was she doing? How was she trying to stop them?"

"I don't know." She shook her head, looking steadily away from Margie. "She shouldn't have gotten involved in whatever it was."

"It was drugs," Lewis said, looking at Ceci. "I know that much. Was there a big shipment coming in? Is that what she was trying to stop? And what did you get out of it? What did you get for turning her in?" He stared at her steadily. "A couple of hits of fent?"

"I'm no addict. I'm clean." She held out her arms, inviting him to look. They were covered with stick-and-poke tattoos she had undoubtedly gotten while in juvie. But there were no obvious injection marks or tracks.

"Addicts are switching to smoking fentanyl," Lewis said with a shrug. "Cheaper, easier, less risk. You get a good high without having to risk needle infections. And without any telltale tracks."

"I don't do fent. Or any other drugs," she told him coldly. "You're just making assumptions based on racial profiling."

"Then I must think that Detective Pat is a drug user, too." Lewis turned and looked at Margie pointedly. "Detective Patenaude, are you a fentanyl addict?"

Margie rolled her eyes. He was being annoying and confrontational, which she didn't think was the best way to get to Ceci. But she didn't want to criticize him in front of a witness, either. Showing a rift between them would not be helpful. Other teams might like good cop-bad cop, but Margie found it was better to work together, staying on the same level, treating the suspect with respect and trying to establish a good relationship. Lewis apparently had other ideas.

"Ceci…" Margie said softly, "A little boy will never see his mom again. I'm never going to see my cousin again, never going to get together over tea and talk about the times we had together here as kids. She's gone. Because someone wanted to deal drugs to kids and she got in the way of it. Have I got it right?"

Ceci's gaze was downward. She nodded slightly.

"Who is the dealer? Is it one of the kids here?"

Ceci shook her head.

"Who, then? And how did Laura find out about it? Did someone come to the house at night when she was supervising? I assume you guys are not allowed to have visitors after curfew."

"I don't know what she saw or heard," Ceci told them unconvincingly, staring off into space.

"How many people in the house are Alberta Warriors?"

She shrugged. "Everyone is affiliated with someone," she said. "If not AW, then one of the other gangs. You can't live in this world without protection."

"Who else is AW?"

She lifted her hands, palms up. "I'm not a snitch. I don't talk."

CHAPTER SEVENTEEN

$\mathcal{T}$hey talked to one of the other supervisors before they left. Mr. Gaetz was an older man, with a day or two's growth of beard on his chin and little hair on top. He was shorter than Margie, which was relatively short for a man.

"Is there any way we could get a listing of what kids are associated with what gangs?" Margie asked.

"We have to respect our residents' privacy. And the fact that most of them are trying to stay away from the gangs they were *formally* associated with. It's very hard to break with these guys once you have been accepted into an organization. We try to help them make that transition, but I'll be honest: Most of them are not able to."

"And we would like a list of what those associations are."

"I'll talk to the director, but I'm not sure that's something we can give you. It violates all kinds of rights and policies."

"We want to solve Laura's murder. And it has something to do with the Alberta Warriors. So we need to know who in this house she might have had contact with that arranged for her death. Don't you think that overrides any privacy concerns?"

He shook his head slowly. "Sadly, no, I don't think so. You may feel justified in riding roughshod over people's rights. They're just kids, after all, and we're talking about murder. But that's not the way it works around here. The kids come first."

Laura would have been proud of him.

Rather than smiling at the thought, Margie kept a stony expression. "You speak with your director, then. See how far this institution can push it before the Minister of Children's Services decides that you are not living up to the terms of your charter and shuts down the house or replaces you. If, in the view of Calgary Police Services, you are supporting criminal organizations and putting these kids in danger, you will be shut down so fast you won't know what hit you."

Gaetz shook his head, looking grim. "I'm sorry you feel that way."

But he didn't buckle under and give Margie the information she had requested.

❦

MARGIE AND CHRISTINA had both made time to go over and visit Moushoom. The modest house that Margie had purchased when she moved to Calgary had been selected in large part because it was so close to the nursing home where Moushoom lived. It was within easy walking distance, so either of them could see him at any time, and she was right there in case of an emergency. But he could still maintain his independence as much as possible.

They spent the time immediately after getting home from school or work to make some bannock. They had a little bit of it while they were cooking, and took the rest, still warm and in a towel, to Moushoom's room.

As usual, the nursing staff had left him sitting in his chair in front of the TV. He looked at the door when Margie knocked and opened it, and his face creased into a grin. "My daughters," he called, and held out his arms for them. Margie and Christina took off their masks and both gave their grandfather warm hugs and touched their cheeks to his, whispering in his ear how good it was to see him again.

Stella pranced around them and would not settle down until Moushoom had talked to her and given her ear scratches and assurances that she was a good dog. He got her to lie down at his feet.

"Shut this off," Moushoom directed, motioning to the TV. "What drivel. Show me what you brought me!" He sniffed the air. "Bannock!"

"Can't get anything past this old man," Margie said happily. Of course, most of the time if they brought him something, it was bannock. He loved whatever traditional foods Margie and Christina were able to make. It had been a long time since Kokum had taught Margie the traditional recipes she knew, and the results were sometimes not what she would have hoped. But the bannock always turned out.

She brought Moushoom's meal tray over to him and unwrapped the bannock. There were butter and jam in Moushoom's tiny fridge, as a treat of bannock was not uncommon, and they munched on the still-warm bread, enjoying each other's company.

"How are you feeling, Moushoom?" Christina asked. "You are looking better all the time."

"Yes, getting stronger," he agreed. "It will take more than a little virus to bring this old coot to heaven's gate."

"I hope so! I'm glad you're getting better. We were really worried when you were on the machine." Margie looked over at the small tank of oxygen nearby, which Moushoom only needed now and then at night, if the regular testing during the day showed that his oxygen levels had dipped down too much.

Luckily, it had been bacterial pneumonia and not COVID as they had feared. The doctor said that long-term damage was unlikely.

Margie waited until after Moushoom had finished eating his

bannock before bringing up Laura. Then, as gently as she could, she introduced the topic.

"Moushoom, do you remember Auntie Gaye's daughter, Laura?"

"Remember her?" He smiled. "You were two peas. Joined at the hip."

Margie nodded. She rubbed her forehead, focusing on keeping her composure. Christina looked at her with wide eyes and squeezed her hand.

"What is it?" Moushoom demanded. "What is wrong with you?"

"Moushoom…" Margie cupped her hands over her eyes for a moment. "Laura is dead. She was killed a couple of days ago. In a park."

His jaw dropped. He shook his head. "How could this happen? Explain to me what happened."

"We are investigating. I can't tell you who or why. I can tell you… that she was forcibly given a drug called fentanyl. And that stopped her heart. It would have been very fast, I'm told."

"Why would anyone do such a thing?"

"Right now, we think it was because of drugs. She was trying to stop some… some nasty guys."

"Do not treat me like a child," he warned. "I might be old—I *am* old—but I am not feeble. You explain to me."

"I think it was the Alberta Warriors gang. I don't have any proof yet, and this is not for public consumption," Margie warned, giving Christina a stern look, "but that's what our intelligence tells us."

"Alberta Warriors." Moushoom leaned back in his chair. "A bunch of hoodlums. Why would they do that to Laura?"

"I think she knew something about a big shipment and was trying to stop it. She was working with kids in a halfway house, trying to keep them away from drugs, away from all of the gangs. But she was a threat in some way, so they killed her."

"I don't understand why kids join gangs," Christina said. "I don't understand why there even *are* gangs. Why can't people just think for themselves and get along together? Why do we need to have gangs that are causing all of this violence and running drugs and guns? Why do people have to be so dumb?"

"Kids—and older people—join gangs for protection. For family. Because it is the only thing they have ever known. The Alberta Warriors are an offshoot of the Manitoba Warriors." She saw a flicker of recognition in Christina's eyes at this name, making Margie shudder inside. She didn't want her daughter to have any knowledge of or familiarity with that gang.

"Manitoba Warriors started as a prison gang," Moushoom explained. "Most of the gangs in prison follow racial lines, and these were Indians banding together to protect themselves. When there are Italian gangs and Black gangs and sp—Hispanic gangs, then the Indians need to do something to protect themself. They need to band together and be strong and united. So they did. And the Manitoba Warriors were the biggest and strongest of the Indigenous gangs."

"And how did they get here?" Christina asked. "Why didn't they just stay in Manitoba?"

"They were too much of a problem in the prison. There were too many of them. So the prison decided to do something about it. To split them all up and ship them to other prisons. So they were transplanted to different prisons in Alberta."

"And became the Alberta Warriors."

Margie nodded. "Yeah."

"And they're not just in the prisons anymore, because they let them out?"

"Yes. They get released, and they do the same thing, banding together on the outside for safety in numbers. And because it's profitable. They can work together to set up criminal ventures that are much bigger and stronger than anything they could do individually. The combination of community and power is really strong, and that keeps them running."

"But it would be better for the community if we didn't have all of this violence."

Margie nodded her agreement. "I'm all for law and order," she pointed out. "But I can understand the draw of family looking out for each other and providing for each other. When you have grown up in a place with so much need and broken culture and families, it is really important to belong to something and to have the assurance that your needs will always be provided for and someone will always have your back."

"But like..." Margie could see Christina struggling with this. "Isn't that what the band is supposed to do? And Indigenous outreach and cultural programs? And we have all of these social programs that are supposed to provide for any medical needs and community kitchens and all that?"

"Yes. All of those things help, and we're trying to build a community that supports each other and teaches us how to be better families and how to hang on to our youth and still teach them the old ways, even if they don't seem relevant. But it's a lot to ask. And a gang is much more immediate and in-your-face. You need something, they'll give it to you. And then you do something for them in return. And they keep you coming back, giving you protection and drugs to feed your addiction, and a substitute family to replace the one that you grew up with—or didn't have when you were growing up."

"In school, the children had to band together," Moushoom contributed. "We had no parents. No adults who cared about us. We had to do what we could for ourselves and each other. It's the same in prison. The weak die. Only the strong survive. And the only way to stay strong is by working together."

He smacked his hand on the arm of his chair, making Stella jump and look up at him in concern.

"And now... they got my daughter."

Margie put her arm around Moushoom's neck and leaned into him. "I'm so sorry, Moushoom. I wish that I had known she was in trouble. We didn't see each other. She knew I was a cop, but she never called me or came to me for help. I'm sorry."

"You could not know," Moushoom assured her.

He started to rock back and forth, and then picked up a chanting rhythm. Margie didn't know all of the words in the chant, but she followed it the best she could, listening to him tell of Laura's days spent with them as a child. About how he mourned the loss of another precious child from the family. He prayed for God to take her spirit back to her ancestors and to make her strong, and the rest of them strong in her memory.

Margie listened to him, humming along with the chant, holding Moushoom's hand on one side and Christina's on the other.

CHAPTER EIGHTEEN

They started for home at a brisk walk. While it was still unseasonably warm, the temperature dropped when the sun went down, and it was several degrees colder on the way home than it had been when they had arrived.

"I didn't know whether we should tell him about Laura," Christina said. "But I'm glad you did. I think it was the right thing to do."

"Well, like he says, he is still strong. We worry about him and how long he will be with us, but his mind is still very strong, and we shouldn't try to protect him like a child." They walked for a minute in silence. "Even if you were a child, I would still tell you," Margie said. "I don't think anything is achieved by hiding the truth and trying to protect people from being sad. We need sad times so that we can be happy the rest of the time. And to help to strengthen us and pull us together."

"I don't like being sad."

"No one does."

As they drew close to the house, Stella's demeanor changed suddenly. She pulled ahead on the leash, casting about for a scent and then, when Margie and Christina started to catch up to her, she turned sideways and tried to push them back and herd them in the other direction.

"Stella," Christina objected. "What's the matter? It isn't time to play. We need to go home now. It's time for homework and bed."

Stella bumped against their legs again, growling when Christina tried to push her away.

Margie's chest tightened. She looked around and pushed her hand into her pocket to find the bright flashlight attached to her keychain. Christina was still trying to negotiate with Stella, and Margie nudged her to stop.

"Shh. Let's look around. See if there is something that spooked her. Trust that her senses and instincts are stronger than yours."

Christina was immediately quiet, her muscles stiffening. Margie found the switch on the flashlight and turned it on. She shone it toward the house, panned back and forth across the yard, and then pointed it at the car. They had just walked over to Moushoom's as they usually did, leaving the car at the house.

Margie saw glittery bits of ice on the sidewalk beside the car.

"Stay here," she told Christina, and walked ahead to the car. Stella barked a warning at her. Margie looked around, staying alert, watching for anyone lurking in the shadows.

Every window in the car had been smashed. The windshield was mostly one big sheet of crazed glass. The others had big holes in them. The broken glass lay in little rectangular pieces, reflecting Margie's flashlight beam.

Margie shone the flashlight at the house again, wary. She didn't see any sign that someone had been inside. The door still seemed to be secure. But her cop training told her not to go in without backup. And Christina and Stella didn't count.

She walked back to them, and they stayed huddled close together, heads on a swivel, taking in their surroundings. Margie took one good look around before raising her phone to her ear, and gave it voice commands rather than dropping her eyes to look at the screen.

Within a minute, they could hear the first siren. Margie shivered. It wasn't that cold out. Not cold enough for either of them to be hypothermic after such a short period of time. But the adrenaline was doing things to her. Her senses were all keyed up, alert for the slightest noise or shadow.

Once they had a few cops there for support, Margie went with them up to the house and checked the door. It was still locked and there were no broken windows at the front of the house. Margie inserted her key into the lock and the other cops went ahead of her, turning on the lights and clearing each room.

Once they confirmed it was safe, Margie ushered Stella and Christina back into the house. Stella was anxious, whining and barking and growling if anyone got too close to her people.

"Keep her on the leash," Margie told Christina. "Just until everything is settled down and we are alone again."

Christina sat on the couch and gave Stella ear scratches, trying to calm her down.

"Who would do that?" she demanded. "That's really stupid. Do you think it was just some random thing?"

"Maybe."

But Margie didn't think so. People who committed random acts of vandalism didn't confine it to one car. There would be a series of cars along one block that had all sustained similar damage. But she had looked around at the other vehicles, and none of them appeared to be touched.

Her phone rang, and she looked at the face. A number that she didn't know and hadn't linked to a contact. It was probably Cruz or one of the other homicide cops who had heard about the incident. She swiped the call and answered it.

"Patenaude."

"Detective Patenaude?" a nervous male voice said tentatively.

"Yes. What can I do for you?"

"It's Alexander." A pause. "Alexander Williams."

"Oh, Alexander. I'm sorry, I was distracted. How are you doing?"

"There was… an incident. A rock was thrown through our window."

"Oh, no!" Margie's mind immediately went to her broken car windows. A coincidence? Doubtful. "Are you okay? How is Quinn?"

"We're okay. Just a little bit scared. I think this is related to Laura. There was a note. Saying to mind our own business." He cleared his throat. "I haven't done anything to anyone. Why would they be telling me to stay out of their business?"

"Have you called the police? I'll send someone over to have a look around and to take your statement."

"Yes. They are already here. But I thought that I should tell you, give you a heads-up."

"Thank you for thinking of me. That's very kind of you. We've had… an incident of our own. Can I call you back after we've had a chance to process it? Are you okay for now?"

"We're okay. No one is going to do anything with all of the police here."

"Okay. I'll call you back in a bit."

When one of the officers who had shown up at Margie's distress call walked into the living room, she already had a pretty good idea of what he was going to say. He produced a brick and a piece of paper.

If you know what's good for you and your family, you'll keep your nose out of anyone else's business. Close the case and go back to your life. Keep investigating, and people you love could die.

CHAPTER NINETEEN

*E*ven though Margie had been warned by Alexander, she was still unprepared for her gut reaction to the note. She couldn't have been prepared for it. Her muscles clenched so tightly that they hurt. She tried to avoid grinding her teeth. Her heart was beating hard and fast and she felt like throwing up.

Christina looked at her, eyes wide. "Mom?"

"It's okay, Christina. It's going to be okay. We've got lots of people here to look after us and make sure that we are safe."

"You don't think we're safe?"

"We're safe, baby. I won't let anything happen to you. These guys are not going to get away with threatening me. They might think they can intimidate me, but they're wrong."

"But you know that they..." Christina swallowed. She scratched Stella's ears and held the dog's face in both hands, avoiding eye contact with Margie. She couldn't finish the sentence, but Margie knew what it was anyway.

You know that they killed Laura.

They weren't just threats. They were not going to stop at a brick through the window and a little vandalism. They weren't just going to make a threat and fade into the background. They were prepared to act.

"Nothing is going to happen to us," she promised Christina. "We'll get through this. Just like we have before."

They had dealt with threats of violence before. With a stalker who they knew had killed and who had easy access to them in the neighborhood. They had gotten through that. They could get through this, too.

Never mind that the Alberta Warriors were an organization, not a lone stalker. They could have men—and women—all over the city, in many different places at once.

Margie had the police force behind her.

She had truth and justice behind her.

"Okay," Christina said, but her voice was not convinced. "We'll get through it."

&

IT WAS ANOTHER SLEEPLESS NIGHT. Christina went into her room and shut the door after a while, but Margie suspected that she was probably just watching movies on her phone, not actually sleeping. But at least she was trying for a semblance of normality.

Detective Jones came over when she heard about everything and installed herself on Margie's couch. Police patrols were driving by the house regularly. Margie was not normally armed while she was at home, but she did not lock her gun away.

She tried to sleep. Jones took watch in the living room and sent Margie to bed. She did her best to sleep but, whenever she managed to drift off for a few minutes, it was into restless dreams of danger, and she would jump awake, heart pounding, ready to defend herself and her family against an immediate threat.

In the morning, she was up earlier than usual, making coffee and trying to figure out her next steps. How was she going to deal with the threats? How were they going to move the investigation forward?

They would be canvassing neighbors for any doorbell camera footage that might show who it was that had vandalized the car and left her the threatening note, but Margie already knew what the footage would show. A shadowy figure in dark winter clothing that obscured the vandal's build, and a hood, hat, or mask—or all three—to hide any facial features. There would be no way to identify the perpetrator.

She didn't wake Christina. They had a standing deal that Christina could sleep as late as she wanted without being disturbed, as long as she got to school on time. Margie would not harass her about sleeping in until two minutes before the arrival of the bus as long as she got there. And today, Margie didn't think school was on the list of priorities. Christina could sleep for as long as she liked.

But she was just pouring herself and Jones each a cup of coffee when she heard Christina's door open. She expected Christina to stumble to the bathroom, bleary-eyed, and then to return to her bedroom again a minute later with perhaps a grumble of greeting, and return to sleep for a couple more hours. But Christina was dressed for the day, her hair neatly brushed and braided. She used the bathroom and then joined Margie in the kitchen, pouring herself a cup of coffee.

"Morning," she greeted in a soft voice.

"Did you get any sleep?" Margie touched Christina's cheek briefly, looking at the bags under her eyes.

"A couple of hours."

"You can go back to bed for a while. You don't have to be up yet."

"I can't sleep anymore. Besides, the bus will be here soon."

"Under the circumstances…"

Christina raised her brows. "I still have school."

"I think today you might want to stay home. While we get this sorted out." Margie looked out the window. "I don't know if going to school today is the best idea."

"Are you going to work?"

"I don't know… I suppose so. I can work from here for a while, but I think I will need to be there for the morning briefing and to coordinate the investigation. I can do some work remotely from here, but I might also need to do some interviews." Margie tried to sort out in her mind what different directions the investigation would go. She wouldn't be able to do everything herself, but the detectives and other law enforcement officers they had access to would be putting all necessary resources into tracking down who had made the threats and making sure that Margie, her family, and Alexander and Quinn were all protected.

Christina nodded. "I'm not staying here alone."

"I'll make sure that you have protection. One of the other detectives, or someone else. We have the support of ALERT on this case and whatever other resources we need to draw on."

"I'm safer where there are a lot of people, though, right? Not just sitting here by myself. I mean… obviously they know where we live. I'm not just going to sit here waiting for them to pick their time. I'll go to school, where I'm surrounded by people. They have a resource officer. Teachers. Other students. It would be a lot harder for them to track me and do anything to me in the school."

Margie couldn't fault her logic. "But you're also harder to guard if you're in a big place like that with lots of other people and multiple exits."

Christina shrugged. "You don't need to guard me," she said. "I'm not letting these people scare me. If they were going to do something, they would have done it last night, wouldn't they? Why threaten us and break the windows instead of actually doing something about it? They could just as easily have been lying in wait in the house. They didn't do that."

Margie had to admit that she had been thinking the same thing. The Alberta Warriors had killed Laura. They hadn't wasted their time making threats, at least not as far as Margie knew. They had just approached her in the park and taken care of business. But Margie and Christina and the others were not a direct threat to them like Laura had been. Laura had known specific information. She'd had something to use against them. Information that could disrupt their operation or be used against specific people in the organization.

So far, Margie couldn't point the finger at any one person. She couldn't prove exactly who had killed Laura. She didn't know the information Laura had known. She was asking questions and knew what she was looking for, but she was not getting anywhere in questioning the halfway house residents. She couldn't use any of the information she knew to justify an arrest.

"We can give it a day or two to see if it blows over and to try to get information on who did this," she told Christina. "You can miss a couple of days of school. Get notes and assignments from your friends and catch up again next week. I would just like to be sure that you're safe."

Christina sipped her coffee. "I'm going to school."

CHAPTER TWENTY

*I*t wouldn't do much good for Margie to lay down the law and tell Christina that no, she wasn't allowed to go to school; she had to stay at home under guard until they had solved the case.

It might take weeks or months to break the case and arrest the people who had been involved in Laura's murder and the threats against Margie and Alexander. She couldn't keep Christina home indefinitely. And Christina was too old for Margie to physically keep her at home. Even if she tried to and left someone there to guard Christina while she went into the office for the morning briefing and to conduct some interviews, she couldn't stop Christina from leaving the house. She wasn't under arrest. She wasn't even grounded. She hadn't done anything wrong.

Margie shook her head. She caught a grin from Jones at Christina's response.

Like mother, like daughter. Margie had been quite defiant during her own teenage years and, while Christina was more stable and had a better relationship with Margie than Margie had with her own mother, she still possessed a strong-willed and independent nature. Regardless of whether it was innate, genetic, or influenced by Margie's upbringing, there was no denying that Christina was her own person. She might listen to Margie's opinion or advice, but she would make her own decision.

Margie took a deep breath and let it out. She took a couple of large gulps of coffee. Too bitter and too hot. It seared all the way down.

"I'll walk with you to the bus stop."

"Seriously?" Christina objected. "I'm not a little kid that you need to walk to the bus!"

"Nobody said you're a little kid. Was Laura a little kid?"

Christina looked at Margie. She opened her mouth to raise another argument, but apparently couldn't come up with a good counter to that.

Laura had been a grown woman. Someone who could take care of herself and who presumably knew that she was in danger. Whatever precautions she had taken had not been enough. Being by herself in the park had not been a good idea.

Christina shook her head. "I don't see what difference it makes."

"Maybe not. But we need to do what we can. I want to have eyes on the neighborhood. I want to make sure that you get on the bus safely and that no one is watching you or following you. It's not a perfect solution, because it won't be hard for them to figure out where you go to school, but at least if they can't follow you directly…"

Christina just drank her coffee. Margie knew that she had all kinds of objections to this approach bubbling up in her brain, but she chose not to express them in the presence of Detective Jones, whom Christina liked and wanted to impress. She would want Katelyn Jones to think she was a smart, independent woman, not a rebellious child.

Christina pulled out her phone and scrolled through her social media or watched videos until Margie was sure that the bus was supposed to be there. She didn't say anything. If Christina missed the bus, she missed the bus. Then she would have to stay home, where they could keep better track of her, or find another way to get to school.

"Okay, I'm heading out," Christina said finally, walking toward the door.

"I'll come along."

Christina didn't object or wait for Margie. She walked at a brisk pace to the bus stop, which was about a block away. Margie looked around her, eyes alert, head on a swivel.

There were the neighbors who had become familiar to her over the last months, out walking dogs and going to work or school. But there were other faces that she didn't know. Indigenous faces, like her own, many of them hidden behind black hygiene masks or bandanas.

Christina didn't appear to notice anything out of the ordinary. She stationed herself by the bus stop sign, looking down the street for the arrival of the bus.

A young man strolled up and stood nearby. Margie moved between him and Christina, giving him the eye. He pretended not to notice.

"Mo-om!" Christina protested in a low voice, expressing her displeasure with this overprotectiveness. Margie stayed where she was.

When the bus pulled up to the stop thirty seconds later, Christina got on board. The man moved to join her, but Margie blocked him. The young man's eyes glittered. "Excuse me."

Margie shook her head. He shifted his feet to get past her, but Margie blocked him more aggressively.

"Are either of you getting on?" the bus driver demanded.

"No," Margie told him firmly.

The bus driver looked uncertain of this. The man eyed Margie. She put her hand on her holster. He took a step back, shrugging. "I'll catch the next one."

The bus pulled out. Margie watched the man rather than watching her daughter's bus heading to the school.

The man smiled.

It was a cool, crisp morning, and he wasn't wearing a jacket. His shirt sleeves were rolled up, showing off his ink.

"Get out of my neighborhood," Margie told him through her teeth. "Unless you want to be arrested."

"For what?"

"Loitering. Harassment. Stalking. Criminal mischief. Whatever I want to arrest you for."

"That's not very neighborly."

"You and the rest of the Alberta Warriors can stay out of my way. I'm not going to put up with your harassment. You stay away from me and my family."

He looked in the direction the bus had gone. "You think I don't know where that bus is going?"

"I'll know if you show up there. Stay away."

He smiled and walked away from her.

Margie watched until he was out of sight and then a while longer. She looked around, noting anyone else who was out of place, and walked back to her house with her hand on her firearm. When she reached the house, Jones was standing on the front step, looking worried.

"What happened?"

She could see the bus stop from where she stood, but obviously could not see any details or hear what they had said.

Margie motioned her back into the house grimly, away from any listening ears.

"Hang on for a second," she told Jones, and called the school and then the police dispatcher to request that a law enforcement officer meet the bus on the other end and make sure nothing happened.

She did not hop into her windowless car and drive to the school to meet Christina on the other end and make sure she got off to her classes safely. Christina would be mortified. And what could Margie do that another law enforcement officer couldn't? It was more productive for her to stay on the case and try to get the culprits at the center of the drug trafficking and murder plot. She wouldn't get anywhere by trying to swat at the flies buzzing around her head.

She dumped her coffee cup and refilled it.

"So what happened?" Jones pressed. "What made you suspicious of that guy?"

Margie shook her head. "Oh, it was pretty subtle."

Jones raised her brows. "Oh?"

"Maybe the fact that he's got AW and 1-23 inked on his shoulders."

"And he wanted you to know it."

"Oh, yeah." It would have been easy enough for him to roll down his sleeves to cover the tats or to wear a jacket. But the whole point of the exercise had been so that Margie would see she was surrounded by them, that they could hang out in her neighborhood and she couldn't do anything about it. So she would see just how close they could get to Christina. Even Christina hadn't understood the danger that she had been in. She had thought that Margie was just confronting a random stranger who happened to want to take the same bus as she did.

Parents could be so embarrassing. Especially parents like Margie, law enforcement officers who thought that they knew everything and that it was their job to patrol the world and enforce everyone's behavior.

"I hope they're taking protecting Alexander and Quinn seriously," Margie said. She took several swallows of her coffee. Quinn wouldn't be going back to school today, would he? He would be staying inside, where they were shielded from whatever Alberta Warriors were hanging out in their neighborhood. And there were probably even more of them there, if Carburn Park was the place they were using as a central meeting hub and exchange site.

"We can call them," Jones suggested.

"Yeah. Yeah, let's do that." Margie pulled her phone back out. It vibrated while in her hand. She looked at the incoming call. Moushoom's care center. Her heart plummeted. First they had tried to harass Christina at the bus stop, and then they were causing problems at the care center too? How had they known about Moushoom? What were they doing over there?

She looked at Jones, panic probably evident in her eyes.

"You take that," Jones instructed. "I'll call to make sure Alexander is being looked after."

Margie nodded her thanks and swiped to answer the call from the care center.

CHAPTER TWENTY-ONE

*M*rs. Patenaude?" the woman from the care center greeted cheerfully. "I'm sorry to bother you during the day."

"No, that's fine," Margie said, taking a deep breath. If the woman's demeanor was any indication, then nothing was wrong. They didn't have some Alberta Warrior over there threatening to shoot the place up. No one had come to take Moushoom away on an imagined outing or take him hostage by force. "What can I do for you?"

"Your grandfather asked me to call you. I tried to explain this to him, but he didn't understand, and he said you would."

"Yes?"

"He got a package in the mail today from one of his other grandchildren. It is a USB drive with some photos or something for him. But of course, he doesn't have a computer, and the TVs in the rooms are not sophisticated enough to have USB ports. I told him that I could put it on my computer to see what it was for him, but we would have to print the pictures out, if it is something else, we would have to find a device that we could use to play it back for him. I thought that you and your daughter might just want to bring a computer with you the next time you visit him…"

It took a while for Margie's brain to catch up with what the woman was saying.

"Wait, let's back up a bit. Who sent this package?"

Margie's mind immediately went to letter bombs, poisons, and other terrible thoughts. But of course, it had already been opened and no one had been hurt. It was just a USB stick with some photos on it.

"I'm not sure who it was from. He has the packaging in his room and the USB doesn't say anything on it. One of his grand-children, I think. We don't know everyone as well as you; most of them only visit once in a blue moon."

"One of his other grandchildren. But you don't know which one? And you don't know what is on it?"

"I was going to check but, honestly, we aren't supposed to connect any outside devices with our computers in case they could have a virus that could damage our systems. I know it's kind of over-the-top, but…"

"No, that's probably the best. Look… can I come over right now and get it? Would you mind?"

"Well, of course not. That would be perfectly fine. I just assumed that you would be at work."

"I'm working from home right now. But I could come over to pick it up."

"Certainly. Just ask for Mirabelle at the reception desk. I'll bring it to you. Or if you want me to return it to your grandfa-ther, I can leave it in his room, and you can get it from him and explain what it is. I think he understood that it might have pictures on it, but when I said it could be a video or some other document or database, he said that you should be the one to look at it."

Margie's heart was pounding. "Yes, he's absolutely right. If you'll just hang on to it, I'll be right over."

She grabbed her laptop and was looking around for her laptop bag to put it into when someone came in the door. She whirled around, her heart leaping and her hand jumping to her gun before seeing that it was Detective Lewis Riley.

"Oh." She blew out her breath. "You startled me. Man. Okay. My heart is fine now."

"Everything okay?"

She gave him a look. Was everything okay? He had to know that everything was not okay, that with her and her family being threatened at every turn, everything was most definitely not okay.

"Sorry," Lewis held his hands up in surrender. "Bad question on my part. I didn't think. I take it that things have not improved since the report of your car being vandalized last night?"

"Not just vandalized. They included a brick with a note threatening my family. And in case you didn't notice out there," Margie motioned to the door and the street outside, "The neighborhood is crawling with Alberta Warriors, which I cannot do anything about. And one of them tried to get onto the bus with my daughter this morning."

"Oh. Yeah, I can see how that could make you jumpy."

"And I just got a call that someone sent a package to my grandfather, and I have no idea what might be on the USB drive that they delivered to him. I don't know how they would even know where my grandfather is. Unless one of them was following us last night, which I guess is completely within the realm of possibility."

Lewis noted the laptop in her hand and nodded to it as Margie found a soft-sided case and slid it inside. "You're going to find out?"

"Yes. And don't try to talk me out of it or tell me that I shouldn't be putting some unknown device into my computer when I don't know what will happen. I'll keep it offline so it can't infect anything else, but I need to know what's on the USB drive right now. I'm not going to wait for a forensic team."

Lewis nodded. "Fair enough. Do you want some company?"

Margie took a steadying breath. "Sure. Yeah."

"Shall we take my car?"

"It's only a couple of blocks away."

"Oh, that's nice and handy. With the neighborhood crawling with Alberta Warriors, do you really want to walk over there and lead them all directly to him?"

Margie stopped and looked at him. "No."

"Hop in my car. We can zip down Deerfoot, make it look like we're going over to Alexander's house, and then loop back around when we're sure we don't have a tail."

Margie didn't have the time to analyze every aspect of the suggestion, but it sounded like a better idea than just walking into the care center with a half dozen Warriors on her tail.

"Okay. Sounds good."

"I'll stay here until we have a plan," Detective Jones said, lowering her phone from her ear. "Alexander is fine and Quinn is staying home. They're not going anywhere until things settle down."

LEWIS WAS a good driver and an effective agent. By the time they looped around, Margie was certain they didn't have anyone on their tail, so she could rest easy that they were not leading the fox straight into the hen coop. The woman at the desk called Mirabelle, one of the nursing aides, who brought Margie the USB drive quickly, not making them wait an extended length of time while she completed other duties. Margie was grateful not to have to wait.

Margie inserted the drive into her USB port and navigated to it on the file system. She did not have the computer set to autorun anything inserted into the port. When she double-clicked the drive icon, she was prompted for a password.

"Do you know what the password is?" Lewis asked unnecessarily.

Margie thought about it. How many chances would she have to get it right? Unlimited attempts? Three? One?

If it was a USB drive sent to her by the Alberta Warriors via Moushoom to damage her computer or get her information, then she had already bypassed that by not allowing it to autorun.

But what had Mirabelle said? She had said that it had come from another grandchild.

What if it had?

"Let's go see him," Margie said, picking up her laptop and heading toward Moushoom's room.

Lewis followed her immediately. "Yes, ma'am."

Margie knocked on Moushoom's door and poked her head in. "Moushoom?"

He was not in the middle of a bath or a meal, but was parked near the TV as usual. His face crinkled into a big smile.

"My daughter!"

Margie motioned Lewis in behind her. "Detective Riley, this is Moushoom. Moushoom means grandfather."

Lewis nodded his head respectfully. "Lewis, sir."

"Sir," Moushoom chuckled. "You got here fast, daughter. I didn't expect to see you here during the day."

"I was working at home, so I thought I would just come over. Do you have the package this came in?"

He nodded and gestured to the garbage can. "It is over there."

Margie pulled on a pair of gloves before picking it up. It was a media mailer, stiff cardboard that could be picked up at any Staples store in bulk. She turned it over and saw that it was addressed not to her grandfather, but to Margie in care of Moushoom. She blinked at that, frowning to herself. She looked at the corner for the sender's address and saw Laura's name hand-lettered. She remembered Laura's neat printing. It hadn't changed in the years since they were teenagers.

She sat down, her knees suddenly weak.

"What is it?" Moushoom questioned. "Are you okay?"

Margie nodded. She tried to speak calmly and clearly around the lump in her throat. "It's from Laura," she said. "And it's directed to me." She checked the postmark to confirm it was mailed before Laura's death, but the imprint was unreadable. She didn't even know if they were dated anymore. Or just some machine-readable marking that the naked eye could not decode.

"From Laura?" Moushoom's expression softened. "What would she have sent?"

"I guess she knew your address but didn't know mine, so she sent it to you instead."

"She sends Christmas cards," Moushoom explained.

"So she had your address on her Christmas card list." Margie swallowed hard and looked at Lewis.

"You still need the password," he reminded her.

Margie nodded. It had been addressed to her, not to Moushoom. Therefore, the password was something that she would know. She opened her laptop back up and tapped the password in. The contents of the drive were listed on the screen.

Lewis's brows went up. "Well, that was quick."

"We had a secret handshake, too."

He smiled.

Moushoom was leaning forward in his wheelchair, trying to see what Margie was doing.

"Is it pictures? Mirabelle thought that it was probably pictures."

Margie scanned through the short list of files. "There is a video. But I don't think I should play it here."

"A video from Laura? Maybe it's of Quinn."

"No, I don't think so. She sent it to me. We hadn't been in touch much recently, and I think it was probably something that she wanted me to look into as a police detective. Which means that it isn't a video of Quinn. It might be something disturbing. Not something I would play for you."

Moushoom scowled. "I am not a child," he reminded her. "I have probably seen far more disturbing things than you have."

She would have agreed with him if she hadn't been a law enforcement officer in Winnipeg for ten years. She was sure that Moushoom had seen some terrible things in his time, especially in his residential school years, but she wasn't about to show him a video that might include torture or murder.

CHAPTER TWENTY-TWO

*D*espite Moushoom's objections, Margie and Lewis returned to his car before playing the video. Margie held the laptop on her lap and angled it so that they could both see it.

As it turned out, there was no need to see the video. The camera was pointed at a wall in a dark corner. It was the audio that Laura had been capturing—a couple of voices discussing the arrangements for the arrival of a large shipment of drugs.

The first time through, Margie tried to make out each word. Some of the conversation was quite muffled. She could get the overall shape of it, but she wished she could understand more.

The deal was to go down tonight, so they wouldn't have a lot of time to prepare for it, if they wanted to disrupt the Alberta Warriors' pipeline right away. There were enough details there to be able to stop and confiscate the drugs. But Lewis was more concerned with being able to get the person giving the orders.

Margie played the recording again. She listened carefully for every clue she could find about who the people discussing the deal were. Unsurprisingly, she didn't know all the players involved. She had only been dealing with homicide since transferring to Calgary and, while some of those murders had been connected with the

Alberta Warriors, they had been lower-level deals, and she didn't know any of the really big players in the organization.

But Lewis had been undercover, trying to get all of the details he could about the Warriors' involvement in drug trafficking in the province for some months, and he would, Margie hoped, have a better idea of who the players were.

The car was cool, but Lewis reached over and turned off the heater. Margie played the recording again and, this time, without the noise of the heater fan, it was a little clearer.

"How did Laura find anything out?" Lewis asked, giving Margie a stern look as if she had been arguing with him about the case. "How would she know anything about the Alberta Warriors and what was coming down the pipeline?"

"Well…" Margie thought about it. "She was working with the kids in the halfway house. A good number of them were Alberta Warriors."

"But they wouldn't have any knowledge of a big shipment like this. They might be aware of what was going on through the juvenile facility, maybe even the halfway house. But in Carburn Park or one of the other parks nearby? How would she hear about that?"

Margie stared at him for a minute, trying to understand what he was encouraging her to see. Then, as she played the audio again, it clicked into place. Her eyes met Lewis's.

THERE WERE two separate police actions, both timed to go down simultaneously so that one party could not tip off the other. As planned, there was a team in place to stop the deal going down in the park.

And downtown, Margie was with Lewis at the halfway house, where he knocked politely on the door some time after curfew. It was a while before the door was opened. They didn't hear yelling back and forth this time. Everybody was, Margie suspected, in their bedrooms with their lights out, so they weren't allowed to go to the front door to take callers. It was Mrs. Craig herself that opened the door.

She looked in confusion at Margie and Lewis. She shook her head.

"What? I don't understand what you're here for. You must know that it's after curfew. None of the kids can talk to you right now."

"We aren't here to talk to the kids."

"What is it, then? Can't you wait until morning?"

"You were very helpful when we were here before," Lewis said. "What has changed?"

"I don't think this is appropriate. You shouldn't be here after curfew. And I don't think I should let you talk to any more of the kids. They can't help you. They're all just working on their own rehabilitation. If they know anything about what happened to Laura—and I don't think for a minute that any of them have any knowledge about it—then you should come back during the day and make sure that they've had a chance to talk to their court-appointed advocates before you start asking them more questions. I just don't like the way you're taking advantage of these kids."

"Or maybe you're afraid they'll pick up on what's happening in the house or slip up and tell us something we don't already know. Like they did yesterday. No matter how careful they are and how hard they try to obey what they've been told, kids still make mistakes and, once the cracks start to show... people like Laura figure out what's going on."

"I don't know what you're talking about," Mrs. Craig said, shaking her head. "Why don't you come back in the morning with a warrant? I'm not required to let you into the house and I don't think it is a good idea. If you are going to bully and take advantage of these kids, I'll go to the papers. I'll go over your heads and report you."

"You mean one of these?" Lewis held up a piece of paper folded lengthwise. The backer was headed "Warrant."

Mrs. Craig's eyes widened. She hesitated, not sure what to do. Slam the door in their faces and hope they wouldn't break it down? Throw out accusations or try to confuse them? Let them talk to the kids and hope that they didn't really know enough to cause anyone any trouble?

"Mrs. Craig?" Margie held out her hand to shake, and Mrs. Craig mirrored her movement, muscle memory responding before her body could process the competing directions from her brain. Margie took Mrs. Craig's hand. "You're under arrest." She snapped a bracelet over the supervisor's wrist and immediately turned her and reached for the other arm. Mrs. Craig resisted.

"No, what are you doing?"

She was too slow to pull back, and Margie had the other bracelet in place. She held Mrs. Craig still and searched her pockets, waistband, bra, and any other hiding places normally utilized by the criminal element.

There was disruption from within the house, kids shouting back and forth. Margie looked at Lewis, bracing for trouble. She guided Mrs. Craig out of the house into the waiting hands of the other law enforcement officers. The others breached the house, hurrying in the door and spreading throughout the house to check for any other trouble. They hoped that by flooding the house immediately with as many LEOs as possible, they could prevent any further violence and protect those who were not actively involved in the gangs from those who were.

One other supervisor was present that they hadn't met on their first visit to the house. Lewis sat her down in one of the cars lined up in front of the house and called in to the members of his ALERT team who were standing by to find out if she had any criminal record or known association with gangs in Calgary or in the rest of the province or any of the neighboring provinces. It would likely take a few hours to be sure that she was clear, if she was.

All of the youth were removed to the police department until they could be cleared and returned, once there were adults who could properly supervise them once more. They were down at least two supervisors, possibly more.

Lewis was talking with Patrick. Margie took on Ceci, hoping to do the investigation justice. Ceci had been put in an interview room by herself, keeping her isolated so that she didn't have a chance to talk to anyone else in person or on the phone. Her phone had, of course, been confiscated for the investigation. All properly papered.

Ceci looked at Margie as she entered the room, her eyes dark and suspicious. She had not washed her mascara off before going to bed, or else she hadn't gone to bed yet. It was smeared and streaked now.

"Is it true?" she asked immediately. "You arrested Mrs. Craig?"

Margie nodded. "She has been arrested for her involvement in the drug trafficking that Laura was trying to stop, and in Laura's murder."

She observed Ceci for her reaction to this news.

Ceci blew out her breath and her shoulders slumped. "Really? It's over?"

Margie nodded. She sat down across from Ceci. "Why don't you tell me what happened? How did you get involved in this?"

"I wasn't involved," Ceci said immediately. "I was trying to get out of the gang. Mrs. Clothier was helping me. She said she could help me to get out and they wouldn't bother me anymore. But…" She shook her head, blinking and swallowing hard. "We couldn't tell her about Mrs. Craig."

"If you had…" Margie didn't finish.

Maybe Laura wouldn't be dead.

"*I* would be dead," Ceci declared. "If any of us had said anything about her…" She just shook her head, choked up, and wasn't able to say anything further.

"Laura was trying to help you."

"You think I don't know that? She was *real*. She meant it when she said she wanted to help. It wasn't just words. But it was too big for her. I knew she suspected someone else in the house

119

was leaking information, but she figured it was one of the other kids."

"But then she figured out it was Mrs. Craig. And she recorded a conversation between her and one of the bosses late at night."

Ceci scrubbed at her eyes with her fists. "She shouldn't have done that. She should have just stayed out of it."

"She wanted to make things safe for you and the others."

"How did you find out?"

"She sent me a copy of the recording."

"She did?" Ceci shook her head. "I didn't know. She said she would take care of things, but I didn't think she knew."

"You knew she knew about the trafficking through the park."

Ceci looked for a way to deny it, then finally nodded. "Yeah. She had seen things going on in the park near her house. She said she knew they were Warriors. She said that if you wanted to stop it, you had to stand up to them. That if everyone stood up and said they wouldn't put up with the gangs and trafficking in their community, they could drive the gangs out." She pressed her lips together, obviously not in agreement. Look what had happened to Laura.

" 'The only thing necessary for the triumph of evil is that good men do nothing,' " Margie quoted.

"She said that," Ceci admitted.

"She believed it. Laura always stood up for what she believed in."

CHAPTER TWENTY-THREE

*I*n Carburn Park once more, Margie watched the small group of mourners grow as they were joined by other members of the community, law enforcement officers who had worked on the case in various capacities, and members of the extended family whom Margie hadn't seen in years. She couldn't identify them all, but she continued to smile at them despite her mask and to give hugs and handshakes despite the risk of infection. At least it was an outside gathering. She didn't think they were breaking any of the gathering restrictions meeting there for the small memorial service.

Christina was in charge of Moushoom's wheelchair and pushed him back and forth between people so he could say hello to all the family members he had been missing. He was clearly one of the social centers of the gathering. At the other nucleus, Alexander and Quinn did not appear to know as many of those who had come to celebrate the life of his wife. But they continued to nod and shake hands anyway, meeting many of them for what would be the first and last time.

Eventually, much later than planned, Margie called for everyone's attention and held the microphone in front of Moushoom's face.

He started with a short introduction, thanking everyone for coming and telling them about Laura and her escapades as a child. He looked at Margie a few times, and she nodded for him to continue. She had to switch the position of the microphone a few times due to sore muscles, but she let him talk for however long he wanted to.

Eventually, he started a smudge, burning herbs on a salver and waving the smoke, offering it at each point of the compass. He chanted in Michif and Cree, flowing from one to the other without any apparent effort. Margie could understand most of the Michif but little of the Cree. More that she needed to learn if she wanted to keep the traditions of her forefathers alive.

He switched to English once more and prayed to the Great Spirit to watch over Laura and guide her to her fathers and her father's fathers. There, she would watch over her husband and son until they could join her someday. He looked at the young people assembled to one side. Not cousins, but residents of the halfway house. He blessed them to be strong like Laura and always stand up for their beliefs. There were tears in the eyes of most of those prison-hardened faces.

Eventually, he was finished. Margie thanked him and invited everyone to stay as long as they wanted to and to enjoy the park Laura had loved and reclaim it from the men who had committed violence there.

She drifted over to Lewis, nodding and not sure what to say to him after the ceremony. She had no idea what he thought of her traditions.

She looked toward the kids from the halfway house. "I'm surprised at how many of them came."

"They really were her kids. They knew she cared about them."

She looked over their faces. "Patrick didn't come. I thought he was one of her special cases. I thought he would."

Lewis's lips tightened.

Margie waited for him to say what he was thinking, but he didn't.

"Do you know why he didn't come?" Margie prompted.

"He's gone."

"Gone where?"

"That remains to be seen."

"You think he's gone to the Alberta Warriors somewhere?"

"I talked to him after Mrs. Craig's arrest. He was in pretty bad shape. Relieved that she was gone, but I think…"

Margie waited.

"*Someone* told them that Laura had recorded their conversation."

"You think that was Patrick?"

He nodded.

Margie sighed. "That poor boy."

"That poor boy?" Lewis repeated. "You feel bad for him?"

"He didn't know how to get out. These kids have been wrapped up in gangs from the time they were young. It was how they grew up. How they survived juvie. How they would survive after they got out. What happened to them is the fault of the adults who used them. The fault of the circumstances they grew up in. They wanted out. They didn't want to be responsible for someone else's death. The death of someone who cared for them. But it was a matter of survival."

Lewis shook his head. "You're more forgiving than I would be."

Margie let out a long breath. "Someday… we'll get rid of these gangs."

LEWIS SHOOK HIS HEAD. "The gangs will always be there."

CARBURN PARK

Carburn Park, located along the Bow River in Calgary, is a sprawling 135-hectare natural oasis that offers a rich blend of constructed and natural environments for outdoor enthusiasts. The park features two man-made ponds, walking trails, and a regional pathway that meanders through diverse habitats, including a riverine deciduous forest, shrublands, and open spaces.

Nature lovers will appreciate the chance to observe various species of fish-eating birds like Belted Kingfishers and Great Blue Herons around the ponds, as well as diving ducks such as Common Goldeneye in the river channel. With its mix of narrow nature trails flanked by lush greenery and fast-flowing river waters, Carburn Park provides a serene escape where visitors can immerse themselves in Calgary's natural beauty

The author recalls BBQ and canoeing at the park with her son's Cub Scout troop, and running to, around, and back from the park while doing half-marathon training.

Did you enjoy this book? Reviews and recommendations are vital to making a book successful.

Please leave a review at your favorite book store or review site and share it with your friends.

Don't miss the following bonus material:
Sign up for mailing list to get a free bonus
Read a sneak preview chapter
Other books by P.D. Workman
Learn more about the author

Get the Parks Pat Survival Pack!

Sign up for my newsletter and receive the **exclusive Parks Pat Survival Pack**, packed with bonus materials and extra goodies you won't find anywhere else.

Stay in the loop on new releases, special offers, and insider content —all delivered straight to your inbox.

Sign up today and start your adventure with Parks Pat!

https://shop.pdworkman.com/products/parks-pat-survival-pack

Here's what's inside:
- **Out with the Sunset (Book 1, eBook)**

Begin Margie's journey with her first gripping case as a Calgary homicide officer in the Parks Pat Mysteries.

- **Out with the Sunset (Book 1, Audiobook – Computer Narrated)**

Take the mystery on the go—perfect for your commute, workout, or a walk through the park.

- **Bonus Prequel Story: *Flight of the Bluejay***

Discover Margie's *true beginning*. Before she was a sleuth, she was a pregnant teen on the streets—fighting to survive and find her place in the world.

- **Discover Calgary's Treasures – Photo Minibook**

Step into the beauty of Calgary with this exclusive photo album showcasing the first 15 parks that inspired the series.

- **Digital Wallpapers**

Bring the beauty of Calgary's parks to your phone, tablet, or computer with stunning photography.

SNEAK PEEK AT BENEATH
THE ICY DEPTHS

BENEATH THE ICY DEPTHS

A Chilling Death

When a woman plunges through the ice into dark, murky waters, everyone assumes it was a tragic accident. Detective Margie "Parks Pat" Patenaude isn't so sure. Something about Julia's death doesn't add up—and as Christmas approaches, Parks is determined to uncover the final clue that will reveal a killer with ice in his veins.

What begins as a winter tragedy soon spirals into a chilling mystery that will push Parks to her limits, testing both her instincts and her resolve.

Tropes You'll Love:
1 a suspicious winter accident,
2 bone-chilling atmosphere,
3 clever detective work,
4 a race against time, and
5 a brisk, satisfying police procedural.

⭒⭒⭒⭒⭒ "The vividly described cold, the icy water that took the reporter's life, and the callous killer that comes looking for

Margie combine to set a supremely chilling atmosphere. I could not look away until the very last word."

Step onto the ice with Parks Pat—read on for chills and thrills.

CHAPTER ONE

$\mathcal{M}$argie was working at her desk. Snoozing, if she were to be honest with herself. The bullpen was warm and Margie had hit her midafternoon slump, trying to push through some paperwork but making little progress.

The phone ringing jolted her awake. She nearly fell out of her chair. She reached for the receiver, looking at the phone number on the display as she did so. The number was familiar, but she couldn't put a name to it until she picked it up and heard the voice.

"Detective Patenaude," she greeted.

"Detective Parks Pat," Gagnon's French-accented nasal voice drilled into her ear. "They're asking for you at this scene."

She knew that Gagnon had been called out to a newly discovered body an hour or two earlier. She had envied his going out, even though she didn't much feel like standing outside in the cold today. At least it was something to do.

"They're asking for me?" she repeated.

"They need your particular area of expertise."

Margie's area of expertise was nothing more than having been called out to attend a few murder scenes at Calgary parks, which had led to her being dubbed Parks Pat, and now she was the expert on bodies found in parks and wilderness areas.

She also attributed it in part to her Métis heritage. It gave her a bit of mystique, with people thinking that due to her European explorer and Indigenous Cree ancestry, she must have some special connection with nature and have learned tracking and lore at her parents' knees.

She was doing her best to learn more about Mother Earth and her secrets from Moushoom, her grandfather, but Margie had grown up a city girl and was woefully bereft of instinct in the area of tracking or even following a map. It was a standing joke how easily she could get lost, even following GPS directions.

But, despite Margie's lack of skills or specialized knowledge, she was the proclaimed expert on deaths in parks, and they would keep calling her out to the scenes of murders or accidents in Calgary parks for as long as she worked homicide in the city. There was no shaking the name and reputation now.

"We're at Bowness Park," Gagnon told her. "You know it?"

"Sure, I know Bowness Park," Margie agreed, happy she was familiar with this one. She remembered visiting Bowness Park as a child on vacations to Calgary. Most of her trips there had been during the summer, when they had enjoyed picnics and BBQs, riding the zip line, and playing tag on the other playground equipment. The couple of Christmases that she had spent in Calgary, they had gone skating on the lagoon in Bowness. There had been fires and hot chocolate, and it had been a lot of fun. Margie had enjoyed skating and had not been bothered at all by her fear of water. Frozen water held no terrors for her.

Boating during the summer was another story. But skating in the winter was a good memory. She had loved spending that time with her cousins and other members of her extended family.

"So you can get out here?" Gagnon pressed.

"Yeah, you bet. I have my car. It should take me about… half an hour to get down…" Margie hazarded a guess, even though she had no idea how long it would actually take.

"Dress warmly," Gagnon warned.

Margie had her toque, gloves, and other winter gear in the car, so that wouldn't be a problem. The weather had been mild the last few days, but she knew it would be colder in Bowness Park than downtown.

"I'll be there as soon as I can," Margie promised.

As Margie stood up and got ready to go, Detective Katelyn Jones was returning to her desk after getting coffee from the breakroom

"Parks Pat is on call," Margie advised Jones. "Bowness Park."

"Have fun," Jones told her cheerfully. "Don't worry about the rest of us, stuck at our desks flipping through dusty cold cases."

"Well, I guess I've got a cold case of my own," Margie laughed.

CHAPTER TWO

*M*argie worried at first that she had taken a wrong turn, it was taking so long to drive to Bowness Park. She didn't remember it being so far west. She had thought it just the other side of Crowchild Trail, but it was a long way past that. The GPS wasn't objecting that she had missed a turn, so she kept going, following the instructions as they were dictated to her and shown on the screen.

Then she did miss the turn into the park. The entrance was well-hidden. Margie swore when the GPS instructed her to perform a U-turn to get back to the park.

After she got turned around and took another run at it, she found the initial descent into the park familiar even after all the years since she had been there as a child. Margie knew she was in the right place.

She spotted a police car in the main parking lot and an officer stood nearby with a black mask, high-vis traffic vest, and orange baton, chatting with park patrons. It was evident that there wasn't much for him to do there. All of the experts were probably there ahead of Margie.

She drove up slowly, waiting for him to finish talking with an older couple before turning his attention to her.

"Detective Patenaude," Margie announced herself after rolling down the window and letting the brisk air in.

"Ah, Detective. You are this way," he pointed the baton to the roadway she should take. "Just keep following it around. You won't be able to miss all of the other vehicles."

"Thank you."

She rolled the window up again. Gagnon was obviously right about her needing to dress warmly. It was always colder near the water and there was a brisk wind.

She followed the road around and, after a couple of kilometers, found the site of the accident.

She had a lot more winter gear in her trunk than she needed walking only from her house to the car and the car to the office. But she always preached preparedness to Christina. A person couldn't trust that the car would always work and that she wouldn't have a breakdown or get into a motor vehicle accident and end up standing at the side of the road or pushing the car out of an intersection. Margie pulled on ski pants, swapped her shoes for boots, put a puffy vest on under her coat, and bundled up with her warmest gloves, hat, and face covering.

She felt like the Michelin Man as she walked to the line of vehicles and the people gathered there ahead of her. She found Gagnon with a couple of patrolmen with red noses and Tim's coffee cups.

He was a heavy man, made to look even rounder with the bulk of his winter jacket. His face mask was pulled down to drink the coffee, and there was frost in his mustache.

He nodded a greeting to her. "I'm sure everyone knows Parks Pat," he said, without bothering to introduce any of the other law enforcement officers to her. "Found it okay?"

"Yeah, no problem." Or only one, anyway. Margie gazed out at the river. While there was ice and snow at the edges, there was still a wide channel of dark water running down the center. Too early in the season for it to be completely iced over. Even when it was, people would need to be careful and know how thick or thin the ice was. She had seen cars drive on the river when it was fully iced in, but she wouldn't choose to walk on it herself. She would stick to the pond, lagoon, or irrigation ditches. Nothing with fast-moving water. She knew enough about the river to respect it.

There were a number of figures out on the ice dressed in dark coats, too far away for her to make out the insignia. A yellow raft had been inflated but sat unused on the ice. Some men in wet suits stood around talking as if they didn't have a care in the world and were completely unaffected by the cold.

"So, what have we got?" she asked.

"Body discovered in the river," Gagnon pointed to a bright fleck of color at the edge of the ice. "Got caught on a log. They're going to attempt to retrieve the body in a few minutes."

"Did anyone see it happen? Do we know who it is?"

"No. Someone walking over the bridge saw it," Gagnon shifted his pointing finger to the wide bridge past the body caught on the log. "They called it in and, gradually, we got everyone out here to discuss the best way to retrieve it. The ice is thick enough over here," he pointed to the larger group of people, "but not out there," he indicated the men in the wet suits. "They are trained in cold water rescue, so this is their thing. I don't know yet whether they will go out in the boat and approach it from the water or see if they can crawl out on the ice and pull it in that way."

Margie shuddered. "Better them than me. I don't think I'll be volunteering to be part of *that* team."

"Wouldn't get me out there either," Gagnon agreed. "I had a friend drown when I was a teenager. Playing on the ice before it was safe." He shook his head. "Ice opened up right in front of me. Water was as black as pitch. Like a gateway to hell."

Margie shuddered, even though she was warm in her winter clothing, at the thought of seeing something like that happen right before her eyes. Or worse, having it happen to her. She could imagine the ice water closing in around her, chilling her to the bone and pulling her under.

"That's horrible," she told Gagnon.

He made one of those indescribably French grunts of acknowledgment. "Oui."

Margie smiled. "We say *oui* too, but we spell it w-i-i."

He raised his brows inquiringly. "What?"

"In Michif. The Métis language. We say *wii*."

"Ah." He nodded. "It is all a bastardized French, is it not? Pidgin?"

Margie resisted the urge to snap at him. He knew something about Michif at least, and was making an inquiry to understand more. It was good to ask questions, even if she didn't like his approach.

"From my understanding of the definitions, it is a creole, not a pidgin."

"Creole like New Orleans?" He shook his head. "It's not the same."

"A creole is two different languages joining to become a new language. A pidgin is a simplified version of a language. Some say Michif is creole and some say it isn't. But it is a mix of French and Cree and some other influences."

Gagnon nodded. "I see."

The men out on the ice began to move. Margie watched the men in wet suits begin to push the raft. But they didn't push it out into the river as she had expected them to. They pushed it along the ice toward the point where the body was caught on a branch or log. Margie and Gagnon watched, both tense.

As the men in wet suits got closer to the body, Margie heard the ice cracking. She looked down at her feet as if cracks might appear there, but she was standing on the shore and didn't need to worry that the cracks in the ice would extend to her feet. Then she looked at the other law enforcement officers and techs standing halfway out. What if the cracks in the ice extended to them?

But they watched, seeming unconcerned. Maybe someone had measured the thickness of the ice and had already established that it was safe at that point. There were a lot of them standing too close together for Margie's comfort, putting a lot of weight on that one part of the ice. She could just picture the shelf breaking off and floating down the river with them still on it.

There were louder pops and cracks of ice under the raft, sounding like gunshots in the distance. There were shouts from the men in wet suits, and then, all at once, the ice beneath the raft broke, and they all slipped into the raft, as graceful as swans, as if that was what they had planned to do all along. Maybe it was.

They controlled the movement of the raft with paddles and poles and snugged it up against the log so that a couple of them could work on freeing the body while the other held the craft in place. Margie was breathing through her open mouth, panting as hard as if she were the one doing all the physical work.

If they went into the water, they would be fine. They were dressed for it. They had trained for it. But she could barely breathe, waiting for them to fall in. Gagnon too was tense, looking like he would grab her if things did not go well. They made a good pair.

Margie blew out a shaky breath and tried to laugh at herself, but the high giggle that came out of her would not fool anyone.

With a great heave, the rescuers managed to pull the body into the raft. They then pushed it away from the log and continued to travel downstream. A few meters farther down, there was a clean shelf of ice. They got close to it, and then two of them jumped out, grabbed the ropes along the side of the raft, and pulled it up onto the ice.

They pulled the raft to the shore, laughing and shouting as if they were having the time of their lives. Margie supposed they were high on adrenaline after tempting fate in the icy water.

Once the raft was pulled to the shore, everyone moved toward it, picking their way through the brush and rocks to reach it and look inside.

"There's your ice queen," one of the men in a wet suit announced. "None the worse for wear."

"Nicely done," said one of the law enforcement officers who had been watching the operation from the safety of the ice. "What about other forensics? Trace on the log? Any other foreign materials caught in the branches?"

"Nothing obvious. Just her and some twigs. Flotsam."

Margie was close enough to see that the man who approached the body first was a crime scene tech she had run into at other sites. She stayed back and waited for him to take pictures and examine the woman's outer clothing.

The victim had obviously not intended to go for a swim. She wasn't prepared for the possibility like the men in the wet suits. The heavy clothing she wore would have pulled her down immediately, dragging her under the water. The icy water would quickly have incapacitated her and made it impossible for her to get herself back to safety. Margie's throat closed as she thought of being dragged under the surface by the weight of her clothes.

The tech muttered to his companions as they examined the body carefully, documenting everything.

"Was her coat torn before you pulled her off of the branch?"

The foremost man in a wet suit shrugged. "It was after we pulled her off."

The tech shook his head in irritation.

Margie thought that the men had done well, considering the circumstances. No one had been hurt or ended up in the water, and they were able to retrieve the body on the first try and not dump her back in the water. All in all, it was a pretty successful venture and not one that she would have volunteered for.

The tech eventually unbuttoned the heavy winter coat to give them a better look at the body.

It was a woman, as the rescuer had indicated. She had long hair frozen into intertwining sticks in a mass around her head. She had a couple of scrapes and bruises on her pale white face. The body under the coat was not slim. Not all of the bulk was the coat —a lot of it was the woman herself. The rescuers must have both been pretty strong to be able to move a woman of her size, especially a dead weight, clothing soaked in water.

The tech described the woman into a hand-held digital recorder, estimating her height and weight.

"She doesn't look like she's been dead long," Margie said. She had seen bodies bloated up in the water, features unrecognizable. Maybe it took longer when the water was so cold.

"No, don't think so," the tech told her after turning off his recorder. "Last night, probably. And she wasn't completely submerged, snagged on the log like that."

Margie nodded. She didn't take out her notebook to note down this information. She would save as much writing as she could for when she was back in her car with the heater on and the doors shut to keep out the wind. Her gloved fingers tingled from the cold despite the layers of insulation she had bundled herself in.

"Any identification?" Gagnon asked.

The tech patted her coat and shook his head. "Will have to check more carefully at the morgue. No obvious wallet. But most women carry their wallet in a purse, not coat pockets."

"No purse?" Margie asked. "Nothing caught on the log?"

"No. Might want to conduct a search downriver, see if it washed up on shore."

❦

Beneath the Icy Depths, Book #12 of the *Parks Pat Mysteries*
series by P.D. Workman
can be purchased at pdworkman.com or at your favorite online
retailer

❦

ABOUT THE AUTHOR

P.D. Workman is a USA Today Bestselling author and multi-award winner, renowned for her prolific output of over 100 published works that span various genres. With a knack for crafting page-turners, Workman captivates readers with everything from cozy mysteries like the Auntie Clem's Bakery series to gripping young adult and suspense novels.

A prolific reader and writer since childhood, P.D. Workman crafts emotionally powerful stories that don't shy away from hard topics. Her books tackle mental illness, addiction, abuse, and trauma with raw honesty and compassion, giving voice to the often unheard. If you crave authentic, character-driven page-turners that hit deep and stay with you long after the final page, you're in the right place.

With each new release, fans eagerly anticipate another thrilling blend of thought-provoking storytelling and relatable characters that define P.D. Workman's brand as an author of unforgettable page-turners—gripping tales that leave a lasting impact long after the last page is turned.

> P. D. Workman, does not shy from probing the deep psychological scars of childhood trauma, mental illness, and addiction. Also characteristic of this author, these extremely sensitive issues are explored with extensive empathy, described with incredible clarity, and portrayed with profound insight.
>
> — —KIM, GOODREADS REVIEWER

Some of Workman's titles have been translated into Spanish, French, Portuguese, German, and Italian.

Workman began writing at an early age and is a prolific reader as well as writer. She is also passionate about teaching and learning, expresses her creativity through art and cooking, and loves exploring the Calgary parks and green spaces where the Parks Pat Mysteries are set. She was a legal assistant for many years and has done extensive charitable work.

Workman was born and raised in Alberta, Canada, and is married with one adult son.

§⋅

Please visit P.D. Workman at pdworkman.com to see what else she is working on, to join her mailing list, and to link to her social networks.

§⋅

If you enjoyed this book, please take the time to recommend it to other purchasers with a review or star rating and share it with your friends!

tiktok.com/@pdworkmanauthor

facebook.com/pdworkmanauthor

x.com/pdworkmanauthor

instagram.com/pdworkmanauthor

amazon.com/author/pdworkman

bookbub.com/authors/p-d-workman

goodreads.com/pdworkman

linkedin.com/in/pdworkman

pinterest.com/pdworkmanauthor

youtube.com/pdworkman

Find P.D. Workman's books at

PDWORKMAN.COM

Scan the QR code below